Secret City

Book I of the Galhadrian Trilogy

Jan-Andrew Henderson

Black Hart Entertainment

Edinburgh. Scotland

Published by Black Hart, Edinburgh 2020
First published Oxford University Press, Oxford 2004
(As Secret City). ISBN-13: 9780192719577.2019
Black Hart Entertainment.
32 Glencoul Ave, Dalgetty Bay, Fife KY11 9XL.

Publisher's Note: This is a work of fiction. Names, characters, places, and incidents are a product of the authors' imagination. Locales and public names are sometimes used for atmospheric purposes. Any resemblance to actual people, living or dead, or to businesses, companies, events, institutions, or locales is completely coincidental.

Cover by Panagiotis Lampridis (BookDesignStars)
Book Layout © 2017 BookDesignTemplates.com

Secret City.
978-1-64826-920-2
978-1-64826-946-2

Faeries, elves, pixies, leprechauns. There are many names for that elusive race of humanoids; the Little People.

Kevin Farmer: *This Strange Planet*

Many of our ancestors lived in constant fear of offending the faeries... they were neither cute nor adorable, but dangerous, vindictive, cruel and not to be trusted for an instant.

Maurice Fleming: *Not Of This World*

Thanks to Katherine Naish, Jem McCusker, Emily Canter and Catriona Wilson

Chapters

The Cup

Warrior and child struggled over the brow of the hill, almost blinded by gusts of freezing rain that tore at their clothes. The warrior swayed and stumbled, trying not to lean on the small figure, for the child was already burdened by a clanking leather bag slung over one shoulder. The man's beard was matted with blood and his breastplate hung half off his chest, bent and ripped, as if it were tin foil.

They splashed, gasping, through a small stream. It was so dark they had not even seen it. The man sank to his knees and his shaking fingers fumbled at the breastplate fastenings until the ruined armour dropped into the mud. Over the storm, and his own ragged breathing, he could still hear the roar of battle drifting up from the valley below. The child looked back the way they had come and shuddered.

"I should be fighting alongside my clan," the warrior rasped. He tried to rise but his legs no longer supported him and he collapsed with a grunt of pain.

"No, Uallabh! We have to keep moving!" The child clasped the warrior's quilted tunic and tried vainly to pull the man to his feet. "We need to get the cup to safety!"

The jerkin fell open, revealing a deep, jagged wound running from the man's shoulder to his waist. The child looked quickly away and saw a faint light seeping into the sky above the eastern hills.

"It will be dawn soon." Tiny hands urgently clasped at the tunic again. "We only have to last a little longer."

An inhuman roar shattered the night and the child's head shot up, scanning the darkness, eyes wide with fear. Uallabh's hand went to the knife at his side and he pulled himself to his knees by sheer force of will. A riderless horse, lathered with sweat and blood, thundered out of the night. Eyes rolling in terror, it swept past them and vanished into the darkness again.

"The creatures must be following us," the man snarled. "You go. I will hold them off."

"They are still in the valley, fighting with your companions. Only one is on our trail." The child fished a silver cup from the leather bag and thrust it at the warrior. "But the one who chases us? A whole army will not stop it."

Uallabh looked down. Miraculously, liquid glittered inside the goblet, almost up to the rim.

"Drink from this," the child urged.

"Never!" The warrior pushed the cup violently away. "I will not be tainted by its dark magic."

"Listen to me," the child whispered urgently. "You are noble and pure of heart, or you would not be here. You will stay that way if you do not attempt to use the powers the goblet gives you. I promise."

"What will it do to me?" the man asked.

"It will stop you ageing."

"I do not wish to be immortal."

"More importantly, it will cure your wounds. I need you!"

Uallabh looked intently at the child, his mouth set in a grim line. Finally, he reached out, took the cup and drank.

There was another horrific roar, much louder now. The child snatched the cup and thrust it back into the bag. Uallabh tried to get up again and, this time, to his astonishment, rose easily to his feet.

"Go north. Hide the magic artefact," the child pleaded. "Then wait for me at the Glen of Roslyn, no matter how long it takes. I will come eventually."

The man picked up the bag and slung it over his shoulder. He now stood fully upright and his eyes were clear and hard.

"And if this… thing kills you?"

"It will not dare risk the Dolorous Stroke. I promise that too."

The Dolorous what, now?

"I have no time to explain!"

"Then I shall, reluctantly, do as you ask – though I curse the day we met."

The warrior took the bag and strode away without a backward glance.

The child crouched down in the wet heather and listened carefully. The sounds of battle were growing fainter but that was a good sign. It meant Uallabh's companions were pushing the monsters back. And the sky was definitely lighter now. It would soon be dawn.

Perhaps everything would be all right.

Then a huge, yellow-eyed figure appeared over the crest of the hill.

The Drummer Boy

Charlie Wilson was a quiet boy. His parents moved around a lot and he didn't have many friends, so he kept himself to himself. He spent a lot of time sitting in his room playing the PlayStation or trying to beat his own high score on some computer game. When he grew up, he wanted to be either a computer programmer or an air traffic controller because he'd get paid a lot to sit and press buttons all day.

"When I was young, I was out having real adventures instead of fooling around with some video game," Charlie's father said.

"When you were young, television hadn't been invented." Charlie snorted. "On the PlayStation, I can have totally amazing adventures. Be anyone I want."

And his father sighed and nodded because, secretly, he thought that didn't sound too bad at all.

He had no idea that Charlie Wilson was soon to have a totally amazing adventure. That, in the process, he would become an explorer, a magician, a detective and a grave robber.

Then, finally, he'd become a killer.

Just before term ended, Charlie came home to find his mother doing handstands in the hall - not that this was anything unusual - for his parents were both professional acrobats. It was a career Charlie found highly embarrassing, so he pretended to everyone that they worked in a bank. He didn't much approve of his parents.

"Guess what?" his mother said, upside down. Her long dark hair brushed the hall floor.

"You found a new way to sweep?"

"Very funny." His mum gracefully flipped back onto her feet. "We've been asked to perform at the Edinburgh International Festival, up in Scotland. There's a whole show dedicated to physical performance."

"You mean it's a circus," Charlie sighed.

"Oh, it's much classier than that - not an elephant or clown in sight." Charlie's father stuck his head out of the living room and waggled his eyebrows. "This might be our chance to get famous."

Charlie had never heard of any famous acrobat and certainly didn't want his parents to be the first - they'd be absolutely insufferable. He was even more horrified to learn they were taking him to Edinburgh with them.

"We certainly can't leave you behind, tempting though it might be." His father patted the boy on the shoulder. "It'll do you good to go somewhere different. Bring you out of your shell."

"What do you think I am?" Charlie grumped. "A mollusc?"

"You'll love it." His mother did a somersault and knocked over the umbrella stand. "We'll only be there for three weeks, but it's the biggest arts festival in the world. There are street performers and jugglers and music and comedy and plays."

"And the bars stay open till three in the morning," his father added. "Not that it makes any difference to anything, mind you."

"We can do family things together for a change." His mother ruffled the boy's thick blonde hair before noticing that her nail varnish wasn't quite dry. "When we're not performing, of course. How would you like to learn to juggle?"

"I'd rather chew my own arms off." Charlie rubbed the pink sticky patch left on his head.

But it didn't matter how much he protested. His parents dragged him to Edinburgh anyway.

In Edinburgh, the City Council had shut down a narrow, neglected street in the old part of the city and erected a huge fibreglass tent in the middle - it stretched from a derelict concert hall on one side of the road to a set of abandoned tenements on the other. (Tenement was an old Scottish word for a tall building, his father explained). This was to be the special theatre where Charlie's parents and other acrobats would perform.

Two workmen stood watching the last of the scaffolding being removed. One was barely out of school, pale and scrawny, with so much acne he looked like he was permanently angry. The other was nearing retirement, skin brown and cracked as an oak door and thin white hair matted with plaster dust.

"Just like a circus big top, eh Jim?" the younger one said. "Only less impressive."

Jim nodded. He had long ago run out of things to say to his companion.

"Hey! You hear aboot Harry?" the teenager continued. He seemed to dislike silence. "Him and the lads were using a wee cellar at the bottom of those deserted flats fur their breaks – it's nice an cosy, know? And out of sight of the boss," he added with a wink.

Jim sighed and leaned on his spade. The youngster took this as a sign of interest and kept going.

"He was foolin about wi one of the pneumatic drills an knocked a hole right through the cellar floor." The youngster sniggered. "An guess what? The lads said they found a tunnel under it."

"Aye." His companion didn't seem surprised. "I've heard stories aboot secret passages under these streets ever since I was wee."

"When wuz that? Nineteen oatcake?" the teenager's gurgling laugh turned into a fit of coughing. He pulled a cigarette from behind one greasy ear and lit it.

"There's a famous legend in Edinburgh." The elderly man continued without a change of expression. "About a bunch of soldiers fixing up the dungeons in Edinburgh Castle, who found a hidden tunnel."

"I didnae hear about that."

"This was two hundred years ago."

"Oh." The youth thought for a moment. "I wasnae around."

"The army wanted to know where this passage went." Jim sighed and continued. "But it was awful small. So they found a wee boy, gave him a drum to bang and chucked him in. The lad crawled through the darkness and the soldiers followed on top, right out of the castle and down the main street."

"Whit happened?"

"After about half a mile, the drumming stopped."

"Maybe he went on strike."

"More likely, he got stuck and died." The older man shrugged. "So the army decided just to forget the whole thing. They hid the tunnel again and now everybody thinks it was just a daft story."

Jim held up a warning finger.

"But late at night, if there's no traffic about, you're supposed to hear phantom drumming coming from below these very streets."

"Load of nonsense." The teenager said cheerfully. "Let's go an get a mug of tea."

"All legends have a grain of truth in them, lad," Jim scolded.

"We'll find out soon enough," the boy grinned. "We told the council about the tunnel and it turns out there's nae official records of it. So they offered us overtime, when this job's over, to have a wee dig under the rest of the cellars. See if we find anything interesting."

"That's a bit odd, eh?" Jim said thoughtfully. "These buildings are pretty old. They must have known about the tunnels back then, but they still built on top of them. And there's no records, you say?"

"Guy from the council told us they got destroyed about the same time the tenements were put up." The boy hefted an identical spade onto a skinny shoulder, impatient to get his tea.

"Nothing left but legends." The old man looked up at the deserted windows, dark and empty as soulless eyes. He scratched his stubbled chin and frowned.

"It's like somebody, long ago, wanted what's under this street forgotten."

The Tunnel

Once he got to Edinburgh, Charlie had to admit he liked it, especially the historic Old Town. It was built on a high basalt ridge leading up to Edinburgh Castle and its tenements and stone spires towered over the rest of the city. Charlie imagined the Old Town probably looked much the same now as it did centuries ago.

There were plenty of things to see and do in a city filled with flowering gardens, ancient courtyards, hidden alleys and vast museums. And Charlie's mother had been right about the festival too. For three weeks, the city was packed with jugglers, magicians, unicyclists, human statues and hundreds of other performers, all dressed in weird and wonderful costumes to promote their shows. All the same, he wished he'd been allowed to bring his PlayStation.

There was one place he did find fascinating and that was the venue where his parents were performing. It was half theatre and half big top, tent-shaped, but made out of fibreglass, not fabric. Like a theatre, its walls were rigid and it had a door rather than an entrance flap. Yet it was as temporary as any circus, erected especially for the festival and destined to be taken down again afterwards. Inside there was no stage or curtains because, as his father explained, this place was specially built for *acrobatic* performances.

"None of your Shakespeare nonsense here, Charlie," his father chirped happily. "No men in tights running around shouting *thou hast killed me naughty knave* and waving plastic swords."

He pointed proudly to the girders, wires and poles that towered above them.

"When acrobats perform, it's a matter of life and death. There's real danger here."

"And that's a *good* thing?"

Charlie's father shrugged.

"Better than working in a bank."

In fact, there was more danger in this particular big top than he could possibly have imagined.

"You can come and watch us practice if you like." Charlie's dad was still staring longingly upward. "Perhaps, one day, you can be part of the act."

"I've already seen you practise," Charlie muttered. He had lost count of the number of coffee tables his parents had broken leaping around their living room. "Anyway, it doesn't look all that dangerous to me. The high wire isn't all that high, is it?"

He jerked his thumb at the rope a few feet above their heads, a crisscrossing mesh dangling just below. "And there's a net."

Charlie's father glanced down at his son.

"That's not the high wire," he laughed. "Watch this."

He took a remote control from his pocket, pointed it at the roof and clicked a button. There was a loud hissing noise and a crack of white appeared, high above in the centre of the structure. The boy flinched.

With an electronic hum, the two halves of the big top roof slid slowly back from the middle, like a huge yawning mouth, until the building was completely open to the sky. There was another hiss and vertical poles, twenty feet apart and with a metal tightrope stretched between them, extended up and up through the gap that had been the roof and into the open air. Now the tightrope looked thin as thread.

"*That's* the high wire," Charlie's father whispered.

"All right," the boy admitted, taking the remote control and inspecting it. "I'm impressed."

His stomach tightened at the thought of his parents balancing so high on the narrowest of supports – but he did like gadgets with buttons.

The theatre was erected in one of the many narrow little roads the inhabitants called 'wynds'. There were dozens of them sloping steeply down from the High Street into an area called the Cowgate – a rundown valley area festooned with pubs, much to the delight of Charlie's father. The boy goggled at the way that the big top was fastened to high buildings on either side of the wynd, rather than being secured by guy ropes hammered into the ground.

"They look like an ordinary bunch of flats, don't they?" Charlie's father pointed to the abandoned and crumbling tenements on either side. "Only, they're not."

"I sense a boring story coming on."

"These tenements were built in front of a gigantic bridge," his dad continued. "They're so tall they made the structure behind almost invisible. This 'South Bridge' was constructed in the 18th century, so horses and carts could cross the Old Town without risking descending the steep slopes of the Cowgate valley. Under the massive arches, hundreds of stone chambers linked by passages were constructed – all easily accessible until the tenements hid them. They were supposed to be used as storage vaults, but people ended up living there.

"Why?"

"Overcrowding and poverty, mainly," his dad replied. "There's legends of people living in deeper tunnels that were dug into the Old Town ridge, even *under* the bridge."

"You swallow a guidebook?" Charlie frowned.

"They called it the Underground City," Charlie's father said solemnly. "Places where the very poorest people got stuck. It was a long time ago, mind you and it's all been built over, so even local people think it never really existed."

His father tapped the side of his nose.

"But I know it does."

"Oh yeah? How come?" The boy was suddenly interested – after all, he'd been playing Tomb Raider for most of the spring - and the idea of hidden passageways appealed to him. Charlie's father looked surprised. It wasn't often he said something his son actually wanted to hear.

"Because the construction crew setting up the big top dug a bit of it up by mistake." He grabbed the boy by one arm. "Come and look at this."

He led his son over to a dark corner of the big top where another door lurked in the shadows. He opened it and they stepped into a short corridor. There was grubby plaster peeling from the walls and wooden slats and bare wires dangled from the roof.

"You can go from the big top right into the abandoned buildings and behind that are the bridge vaults themselves." His father opened a second door and ushered Charlie through. "It's like walking back in time."

They stood in a musty chamber with a low roof and uneven brickwork. It looked very, very old. The vault contained a pile of shovels and drills, a folding table covered in dirty cups and a large portable generator, which gave off an evil hum and smelled of burnt toast. The theatre construction crew had obviously used the little cellar to store their equipment and have tea breaks.

Charlie's father moved a mop, bucket and some plastic safety helmets stacked against the side of the generator. On impulse, he tried juggling three of the helmets but one bounced off the roof and hit his son on the head.

"Sorry, Chaz," he apologised. "Ceiling's a bit too low for that."

Charlie wasn't listening. Behind the mop and helmets was a ragged hole in the ancient brick wall. In the dim light of a makeshift bulb, swinging from the storeroom ceiling, he could see there was a tunnel below.

"Is that…"

"Part of the Underground City? I think it has to be." Charlie's father switched on a lamp attached to one of the safety helmets and shone it into the hole. A narrow, moss-lined passage stretched into the distance, as far as the beam could reach.

"I bet nobody's been in there for a hundred years or more." He knelt beside Charlie and looked into the passage. "It's way too small for any of the workers to fit inside. Have you seen how many sandwiches these guys eat?"

He stood up and began to practice juggling with the helmets again.

"I hear Edinburgh Council wants them to excavate the place properly but we'll be back home by then."

The boy stuck his head into the hole. There was a stale smell, similar to the one inside his parent's fridge. His mother and father weren't too big on cleaning.

"I bet I could fit in here." Charlie waved his hand about in the empty space.

"Don't even think about it." His father dropped the helmets with a crash. "I heard a story in the pub about a little boy who was forced into one of these abandoned passages and never came out again. They say you can hear his ghost drumming under the ground. I forget why he had a drum in the first place."

He scratched his head.

"To be honest, I don't remember much about that entire night."

He put the mop and helmets back to hide the hole once more.

"But there's no way you're going in there. God knows what trouble you'd get into."

Charlie's father was sure his son had no intention of venturing anywhere near the tunnel again. He'd rather sit in his room and play video games than have a proper adventure. He forgot that Charlie hadn't been able to bring his PlayStation with him.

The boy had already made a fateful decision. If he couldn't play Tomb Raider in the comfort of his own home, he would give the real thing a try. After all, it was better than wandering around Edinburgh on his own. He might even discover treasure in the tunnel or find a gold mine or something!

If Charlie had thought more carefully about his computer games, he would have realised there is a sort of rule regarding hidden treasure.

Wherever you find buried riches, you are also likely to come across something horrible guarding it.

The Juggler

Visiting a new place has an odd effect on people. Perhaps it's because nobody knows who they are, or their routine is changed, or maybe the air is just different. Whatever the reason, they sometimes find themselves acting quite out of the ordinary. That's exactly what was happening to Charlie Wilson. The very next day, he got up long before his mother and father, then went down to breakfast on his own. The family were staying at a local guesthouse and it was so early the boy was first into the little dining room. The walls were covered in tartan wallpaper and faded pictures of funny shaped birds.

"Hello there, sonny! Would you like a wee spot of Scottish breakfast?" A plump waitress with a beaming smile appeared at his table.

"Scottish breakfast?"

"Aye. Bacon, sausage, fried egg, fried tomato, fried bread, mushrooms, potato scone, black pudding, fruit pudding, haggis, hash browns, beans, chips, tea, toast and jam."

"Do you have any Weetabix?" Charlie swallowed hard. "I was hoping to be able to move today."

"We've got porridge." The waitress didn't bat an eyelid. "It's grey and lumpy. Just like Weetabix."

"I'll have a glass of orange juice, thanks."

Charlie's parents thought of themselves as rather modern, as well as being very busy, so they allowed their son to pretty much come and go as he pleased. They had given him a mobile phone in case of emergencies but were sure he would never talk to strangers or go anywhere that looked even slightly dangerous.

"We should be thankful he's so ordinary, I suppose," Charlie's mother said to her husband. "When I was younger, I got into all sorts of scrapes, as you know."

"When you were younger?" Charlie's father sighed. "We got thrown out of the pub last night after you did the splits while hanging from a light bulb. But you're right, our son's not like us. He's a sensible chap."

Which shows you that even parents can be wrong. After breakfast, Charlie headed straight for the big top, intent on exploring the mysterious tunnel.

His father had given the boy a key to the theatre, in case he wanted to come and watch the rehearsals - acrobats couldn't exactly climb down from their trapeze to answer the door.

Charlie, however, had no desire to see his parents go through their act. He was convinced that, one day, they'd fall and break every bone in their bodies. But he knew the big top was deserted in the mornings. His parents hated to get up early and Charlie supposed that all performers were the same.

As soon as he was inside the big top, he made his way to the shadowy door at the back, crossed through the abandoned building and entered the bridge vault. He moved the mops and buckets away from the passage, took one of the construction helmets, switched on the light and fastened it on his head. It was far too big, but Charlie's thick hair acted like a cushion, which stopped the hard hat falling over his eyes.

He looked into the tunnel opening. The passage was damp and dark and he had no idea what was at the end of it. There might be a cliff or a bogeyman or, worse, the tunnel might get smaller and smaller until he found himself trapped forever. On the other hand, there might be some sort of forgotten fortune down there, like the stuff they found under the pyramids. What sort of super-computer could he buy then? It might be nice to own a yacht.

He put one arm tentatively into the dank opening and a cold draught raised goosebumps on his flesh. He shivered violently all over.

"Who do I think I am, Indiana Jones?" Charlie withdrew his arm and backed away from the hole, shaking his head. "I wouldn't crawl down there if my life depended on it!"

He stood up and hurried back to the big top, still trembling from his sudden attack of the heebie-jeebies.

"I'll find a computer game store instead," he muttered. "See what the latest releases are."

He stopped in surprise, halfway to the outside door. "Oh… eh. Hello."

In the middle of the theatre, shrouded in shadow, stood a girl in a short velvet dress. She was juggling. Not three balls or four, but six or even seven bright green orbs, glittering intermittently as they spun around her back and over her head.

"Hi there," the girl turned and spoke without missing a beat. "My name is Lilly."

She looked a little older than Charlie and her eyes and dress were as bright and emerald as the balls.

"I'm Charlie," the boy said awkwardly. "I didn't think anyone performed here in the morning,"

"I'm not a performer," the girl replied, her hands a blur of motion. "But my father's a magician. I'm practising to be as good as him."

"Really?" Charlie pointed to the spinning balls. "That's not magic, though, is it? It's just juggling."

Lilly arched an eyebrow and let her arms drop. The balls scattered across the theatre floor, like startled frogs, vanishing under the audience chairs.

Charlie grimaced. Perhaps that hadn't been the right way to start a conversation.

"My parents are one of the acts here too," he said pleasantly, trying to begin again. "They're acrobats."

The girl nodded as if she already knew.

"Do you think you'll ever be as good as them?"

"Me?" Charlie laughed awkwardly. "I don't want to be an acrobat."

"I suppose." Lilly squinted at a trapeze hanging from the roof. "It must be frightening up there."

"It's not that I'm afraid," the boy retorted quickly, embarrassed by the misunderstanding. "I don't see the point in doing something dangerous, just for the sake of it."

"Is that why you decided not to explore the tunnel?"

"What?"

"I've seen it too," the girl gave a sly smile Charlie didn't much like. "In the abandoned buildings at the back of the theatre. It's very dark."

The boy felt himself go red.

"What makes you think I'm interested in exploring some stupid tunnel?"

"You've got a hard hat with a light on your head."

"Yeah. Well, I *was* going to check it out," he blustered. "I… eh… just came back to make sure the theatre door was locked."

"It is." The girl walked over and straightened his helmet. "I'll keep an eye on the place, don't worry."

"Oh. OK then." At a loss for anything else to say, Charlie headed back to the storage vault.

He hunkered down beside the generator, staring into the tunnel once more. Surely he wasn't going to go in there, just so he could prove to some weird stranger he wasn't scared?

The boy thought about his parents. He had genuinely never understood why they wanted to risk their lives swinging high above the ground. He asked his father once and the man had laughed gently.

"I don't want to grow dull and fat working as some salesman, Charlie," he explained. "You're only alive once, so you may as well really live."

The boy hadn't agreed. If life was so precious, what the hell was the point in jeopardising it? Besides, his father had been very clear that he wasn't to venture into the hole.

Only, he really wanted to know what was in there. Besides, the girl had practically dared him to go and she was undeniably pretty. His dad might secretly be proud that he was taking such a chance and, if he got into bother, he had his mobile phone.

The scales tipped. With a deep breath, Charlie knelt and slid, headfirst, into the tunnel.

The air was musty and the moss on the walls surprisingly dry and spongy, which made crawling easy. After a few dozen yards, he realised the little passage was beginning to widen. After thirty feet, the tunnel opened onto a chamber, this one large enough for Charlie to stand. A large archway cleaved the far wall with another passageway beyond.

"Woah! I really am in the Underground City."

He looked around in awe. The flashlight on his helmet lit up an ancient, curved roof, dripping with thin fingers of hardened salt.

"This is well and truly the stupidest thing I've ever done."

He might be taking a chance, but Charlie Wilson wasn't stupid. He took a piece of chalk from his pocket (he had bought a packet especially the day before) and marked a crumbling but readable number 1 on the chamber wall. Then he set off down the new passage. He passed several openings into vaults of different sizes and the tunnel itself twisted left then right, other passages leading off like branches. Every time he took one, Charlie chalked another number, so he'd be able to find his way back.

"Lara Croft was never smart enough to do this," he said proudly, before tripping and falling flat on his face. The mobile phone flew out of his shirt pocket and bounced into the dark. As Charlie scrabbled after it, his helmet bumped against the stonework and one outstretched arm vanished into a cavity between wall and floor. He withdrew it with a shriek, just in case some big rat or land octopus was lurking inside.

"For goodness sake!" he panted once he had calmed down a bit. "How many hidden holes are in this blasted place?"

He sat up and played the headlight over the little opening. It was no more than a few feet long, obscured by dirt and loose rubble.

"That's just great! I couldn't have aimed the phone down there if I was a champion darts player. How am I going to explain losing it to mum and dad?"

The answer, of course, was that he couldn't. He was going to have to try and rescue his mobile. The hole was half-hidden behind bricks and short straps of wood and Charlie began to move the debris to see if he could make a space big enough to reach into. Soon, he realised the gap was going to be large enough to fit his head and shoulders through and, though he really didn't like that idea, it meant he could see where the mobile had gone. After a few moments of cursing, he clenched his fists and stuck his head into the hole.

"Would you look at that?"

The light on his hard hat lit up a stairway, leading down into the darkness. His mobile phone must have bounced all the way to the bottom. Charlie was aware that, bit by bit, he was going further than he had ever intended.

"I'm brave. I'm brave, I'm brave. My mother and father are brave and I can be brave too," the boy chanted, fastening the helmet strap tighter with trembling fingers. "Who am I kidding? I'm just a lot dumber than I thought."

He crawled through the widened hole, got unsteadily to his feet and made his way cautiously down the stairs.

At the bottom was another passage, with an uneven floor that sloped gently downwards. Charlie found his phone then, on impulse, carried on down the hill.

Despite himself, the boy was thrilled as well as frightened. He was finally beginning to understand how his parents must feel, swinging around on their trapeze. He was a bit disappointed, in fact, when the tunnel eventually opened out into a large vault, which seemed to signal the end of his journey. Charlie swung the light around but the doorway he stood in was both entrance and exit to the chamber.

The vault wasn't completely empty. A pyramid-shaped wooden frame and rusty iron hook leaned against one wall, there was a mound of rocks in the far corner, and a waist-high circle of stone in the middle. Charlie walked over to the brick circle and bent his head to shine the torch down. The beam lit up a thick layer of ash and lumpy grey remains of what must have once been coal.

"Looks like someone's been having a barbeque." Charlie raised an eyebrow. "Wouldn't be my choice of place for a picnic."

He turned and walked towards the smaller pile of stones. Though it was no more than a heap of rocks, it looked like it had been put there deliberately. He hesitated for a few seconds, then threw caution to the wind.

"The last time I came across a pile of stones, it was hiding something." The boy bent down and began to remove the rocks. "Doesn't seem right to come all this way and not see what's under this lot. Especially if it's a bag full of jewels."

The stones were piled on top of a rotting wooden board and, once Charlie had uncovered most of the plank, he slid it aside. Underneath was a blackened hollow cylinder of metal the size of an oil drum - it looked like it had been rammed into a hole in the floor. Charlie peered inside and a grin spread across his dusty face. At the bottom of the cylinder was a square object wrapped in dark cloth. It looked like it might be some kind of box.

"Treasure!" he breathed. "About time too."

Lying flat on the floor, he reached into the metal lined hole, grasped the coarse cloth and pulled it towards him. It was certainly a package of some kind, wrapped in the crumbling remains of what seemed like a huge leather glove. With shaking hands, the boy unpeeled the covering. Inside was a tatty book with a faded velum cover.

"Jeez. If I wanted to read something, I'd have gone to the library."

He gingerly opened the fragile cover and a slip of folded paper fell out. He couldn't tell from the light of the torch but he guessed it was yellow with age, for it crackled when he picked it up.

"A treasure map! Of course!" He unfolded the paper and bent his helmet closer to see what was written there. The words were hand-scripted but the letters were large and thick. It was easy to make out, even in the dim torchlight.

If you are reading this you are in mortal danger. Take the book, leev now and cover your tracks. I pray you are brave at hart and of good caracter and, if so, read on then do what you must. Hopefully, at the end, you will find a way to emerge victorious.

Charlie sat bolt upright.

"Mortal danger?" he gasped. "What does it mean, mortal danger?"

Then the tapping began.

It was soft and faint, as if the sound came from a long way down, somewhere under the floor. Charlie's eyes widened and he sprang to his feet. The rapping was growing louder and it was getting faster too. Though it still sounded far off, there was no doubt in the boy's mind.

The noise was heading this way.

Blood drained from Charlie's face and his bravado evaporated. He began to back out of the vault, stuffing the book into his shirt as he went. The rapping was more like drumming now, much louder and definitely heading in his direction. And it was approaching fast.

Charlie Wilson turned and ran.

His journey back to the surface was little more than a blur, for the terrified boy ran as he had never run before, breath hammering in his ears and the light on his head swirling sinister shadows across the passages. The chalk marks flew past, five, then four, then three, then two, then one. He sped through the corridors, bouncing off walls and stumbling over loose rocks. He plunged back into the little tunnel, ignoring scrapes on his hands and knees, as he frantically scrambled the last hundred yards. He didn't slow down until he had burst into the tool-filled vault and every mop, bucket and teacup had been piled back in front of the tunnel entrance.

Charlie took the helmet from his head and placed it on the vault floor with the others. His hands were shaking so badly, he could hardly switch off the light. He sat on the floor, his chest heaving.

"Thank God I didn't have the full Scottish breakfast," he panted. "I'd still be down there."

He got unsteadily to his feet and opened the door leading back to the theatre.

"Nobody and I mean nobody, will ever make me go back into that tunnel," he promised, taking one last look at the covered up hole. "I'll never set foot in that place again as long as I live."

But, though he meant every word, Charlie Wilson couldn't have been more wrong.

The Book

Lilly was still juggling when Charlie staggered back into the theatre. He could have sworn for a second that she had at least a dozen balls in the air and what looked like a couple of mice as well. At the sound of the boy's wheezing, the whirling objects vanished into some hidden pocket performers always seem to have.

"Ah, you're back." Lilly smiled innocently. "Anything interesting down there?"

"Interesting?" Charlie slapped at his jeans and a cloud of white dust rose into the air. "I heard the ghost of that little drummer boy! The one that's supposed to haunt the place. My heart almost stopped."

He began to tell Lilly about the escapade but, to his annoyance, the girl started to laugh. She held up a hand to stop him.

"Charlie, Soon there's going to be a group of council workmen digging under the tenements, from the opposite side of the bridge," she chuckled. "You probably heard them drilling an entrance."

"Sounded like drumbeats to me," the boy scowled. "I've never been so scared."

"A phantom drummer, eh? You should have stuck around. The rest of the band might have turned up."

Charlie ignored her sarcasm and pulled the book from under his shirt, releasing another cloud of dust.

"Anyway, I found this."

"Really? Let me see."

Charlie handed the book over and Lilly opened it.

"It's handwritten and the date inside the cover says 1824." She turned a page and read a little more. "It's the journal of somebody called William Makepeace."

"Like a diary?"

"Exactly."

"Is it a joke? Some kind of hoax?"

"There are parts of the Underground City that have been sealed for almost two centuries and this book's definitely old." Lilly shook her head. "See how dry the paper is."

She peered over the top of the pages.

"What are you looking so unhappy about?"

"I suppose this is real too?" The boy unfolded the note and handed it to Lilly. "It was stuck inside the front page."

"It's the same type of paper." She read the message and looked up at him, eyes sparkling. "This is great!"

"Yeah. Fantastic. Especially the part about me being in mortal danger." Charlie pointed to the offending sentence. "What do you think it means?"

"Don't you see?" Lilly said excitedly. "The note's a warning to stop people going any further."

"It worked then," the boy snorted. "I came back soon as I read it."

"But think! Why would anybody leave a note like that?" Lilly waved the offending scrap of paper under Charlie's nose. "I bet it's cause there's something really important hidden down there. And only the stout of heart will be able to find it!"

She nodded as if this made perfect sense.

"That note's a warning but also a clue, see? There's something valuable right under our feet!"

A look of horror crossed her face.

"What if those council workers head towards it?"

"The speed most council workers work, they'll never get there."

"You said the note was inside this book." Lilly was obviously swept up in her grand idea. "Maybe the book says where the treasure is buried."

"You are getting totally carried away." Charlie held up his hands. "It's just some old diary, that's all. We should give it to a museum before it gets damaged."

"Well, we *could* do that." Lilly smiled a dazzling smile. "But it wouldn't do any harm to read it first. Eh? Where's your sense of adventure?"

"I left it in the tunnel."

"Look, it would only take a couple of days to finish. If there's nothing about treasure, you can hand it over to anyone you like."

"And if there is?"

Lilly shrugged. "Then... we can decide what to do next!"

"What the hell." The boy gave a sigh of exasperation. "Since you've got it all worked out, I may as well give it a try."

"C'mon, Charlie." She gave him a nudge. "It is quite exciting."

"Didn't they write really dull books in those days, with big, long sentences?" Charlie took the diary back from Lilly and opened it. "I'm not really into reading. I like video games."

"What have you got to lose?"

"I suppose." He scanned the first page, scowling with concentration. His frown deepened as he read out loud.

This iz the jurnal of myself, William Makepeace aged about twelve, (tho I am not sure which year I was born, for I am an orphan) in which I am determinned to tell of my life and adventurs, since it is my grate desire to someday write a book of true importanse.

"I knew it!" Charlie groaned. "I've written school essays that were shorter than his first sentence. And who taught him to spell?"

"If he was an orphan in the Underground City, he probably taught himself." Lilly arched a sarcastic eyebrow. "Think you could do that?"

The boy ignored her and began to read again.

I lived in the Canongate poorhouse until I found I was to be apprentised to MacPherson the Sweep – who wuz well known for ill treetment of boys in his employ. He would send them up the narrowest chimneys and, shood they become stuck, would lite fires under them to perswade them out.

"Ouch!" Charlie paused. "He's got to be making this up. Nobody's life is this bad."

"In those days, everybody's life was that bad. Unless they had money."

"I guess some things never change." The boy smiled thinly and began to read again.

One nite I escaped by leeping from the poorhouse roof into a drift of snow and remained buried until after dark. Finally, half dead with cold, I made my way to the Underground City where all manner of criminals reside, and now make my living by means that I am ashamed to menshun...

"Wow." Charlie looked up from the book in astonishment. "This guy's had a hard time of it and I'm only on the first page. I wonder what he did that he's so ashamed of."

"Read the journal. You'll probably find out."

"It's too difficult." The boy protested. "I'll never get through it."

"Everyone has a story worth hearing," Lilly said. "You just need to be able to picture it." She held out a fist. "Maybe I can help."

She uncurled her fingers, blew across her palm, and a cloud of glittering dust circled the boy's head.

"What are you doing!" Charlie waved his arms about, scattering the shining haze. "I got asthma, you know!"

"It's imagination. To help you read the book."

"It's glitter, Lilly." Charlie held up a sparkly hand in disgust. "Now I look like a girl."

"As you were so quick to point out, I'm only a juggler." Lilly shrugged. "What do you want me to do? Pull a rabbit out of my…"

"I'll read the book. All right?" The boy stuffed the journal back inside his shirt. "I'll let you know how far I've got by tomorrow. Where do you stay? What's your phone number?" He tapped his shirt pocket proudly. "I have a mobile. It's a Samsung."

The girl gestured around the tent.

"You can find me right here, every morning."

"Suit yourself." Charlie went to the door and unlocked it. He paused and turned back.

"See this mortal danger stuff? Just what kind of mortal danger do you think…?"

But Lilly was gone.

The Graveyard

After dinner at the guesthouse, Charlie's parents got ready to go to the big top and perform their act.

"Do you want to come and watch?" His father was pulling on a pair of yellow spangled tights.

"I think I'll stay in and read," Charlie shook his head. "Ehm. You're not going to walk through town dressed like that?"

"Don't worry, Charlie, everyone will be staring at your mother." Charlie's mum appeared to be wearing nothing more than three ostrich feathers. "And you don't need to wait up - we might go for a drink after the show. That's if we don't plunge to our deaths from the high wire. Hah. Only joking."

As soon as his parents were gone, Charlie pulled the diary from his bag, flopped onto his bed and began to read. William Makepeace had close, shaky handwriting and that made his long and badly spelt sentences even more difficult.

My best frend and constant companyun is a boy a little older than I, Duncan MacPhail, who it was my grate fortune to meet, for his strenth is admirable, his bravery beyond question and it was he who perswaded me to give up my dishonorable profeshun.

Charlie felt his eyes drooping already. Hadn't this kid ever heard of full stops? He tried to remember what Lilly had said about using his imagination and concentrating on the story rather than the words. And Charlie had to admit, he wanted to know what this William Makepeace did that was so terrible, apart from not learning to punctuate sentences.

He looked at the book again.

I was sitting in Greyfriars Graveyard the first time I met Duncan, a fine spring day when the trees were heavie with white and pink blossums.

Charlie tried focussing on what the writer was actually saying. He pictured ornate gravestones and stately trees ruffled by a cool spring breeze.

Then the strangest thing happened. In his head, he could suddenly see a small boy sitting on a flat tombstone and writing in a book…

William Makepeace looked up as a scented blossom drifted past his head and landed on the velum covered journal balanced between his scrawny knees. Two hundred yards away, through the scattered gravestones, he observed a group of mourners in black frock coats and tall stovepipe hats, attending a funeral. The boy watched them out of the corner of his eye, then quietly opened the book. He took a quill pen and inkpot from his pocket, dipped in the nib and carefully made some notes.

A shadow fell across the flat tombstone on which he sat and he looked up in surprise. Three angry-looking youths, one holding a stout club, stood over him – their burly forms blocking out the sun.

"We know what you're up to, urchin." One of the youths slammed his stick down on the flat stone an inch from the boy's knee. The mourners did not look round. "You're going to wish you'd never set foot in this graveyard."

"I'm already convinced it was a bad idea," the boy said pleasantly, shutting the journal. "So I'll be on my way, gents, and we'll say no more about it."

"Think you're clever, don't you?" The largest of the three boys nodded to his ragged companions. "Grab his arms. I'm going tae teach this wee sod a lesson."

As the toughs moved forward to seize the boy, they heard a cough from behind a nearby tree. A tall youth stepped into the sunlight.

"I dinnae think that three big lads against one wee one is fair, no matter what he's done," the stranger said calmly.

His hair was long and black and a thick tartan plaid was draped over his shoulder then fastened round his waist with an ornate pin. His strange attire marked him out as a highlander- not a common sight in a city which still treated the fierce clans of northern Scotland with fear and mistrust. He kept himself between the sun and his assailants, making his features difficult to see.

"This is no your fight, friend." The largest youth stepped forward menacingly, shading his eyes with one hand. "Go about your business and leave us to ours."

"I don't mind if he joins in," William Makepeace said nervously. "In fact, I think it would even up the odds nicely. If he…"

One of the gang lashed out, the back of his calloused hand catching Makepeace a glancing blow on the temple and knocking him off the tombstone. Without a second's hesitation, the highlander launched himself forward, head down and arms spread wide. His shoulder crashed into the gang leader's chest and outstretched fists slammed into the stomachs of the henchmen on either side. Next moment, all three toughs were on the ground, gasping for air and the highlander was standing above them, brandishing the stick. In his other hand, a small but deadly looking knife had appeared.

"Go on, get out of here, afore I cut ye." He motioned towards the cemetery's iron gates, and the gang got unsteadily to their feet and ran. The knife vanished into the highlander's tunic as he helped the diminutive boy to his feet.

"Up ye get, wee man." He bent down and retrieved the fallen book. "Are ye all right?"

"I'm fine, thank you, and most indebted to your good self for saving me." The boy held out his hand. "My name's William Makepeace, but my friends call me Peazle. So do my enemies, for that matter. I obviously have quite a few."

The highlander shook the proffered hand.

"Duncan MacPhail from Aftonhouse. I dinnae have any enemies." He smiled. "At least, no alive."

"Then I'll count you a friend," Peazle said evenly. "May I have my journal back?"

"This is a funny kind o book now, isn't it?" Duncan opened the journal and looked at the first page. "I've been watching ye write in it and yet there's nothing here."

He flicked through the remaining pages.

"Until you get tae the back, that is. Then there's a map of the kirkyard." He motioned to the crowd of mourners, clustered round the open grave like unhappy shadows. "And you've made a wee tick, marking the spot where that funeral is taking place."

"It's my hobby," the boy said casually. "Funeral spotting."

The highlander's eyes narrowed.

"It's my guess that you work for the Resurrection Men and that's why thon wee gang wished you harm." He looked at the stout stick, then back at Peazle. "I've heard stories of sic a thing - but never really believed they were true."

The Resurrection Men were the most despised of the city's many criminals, for they stole bodies from graveyards and sold them for unscrupulous anatomists at Edinburgh University to experiment on. To avoid suspicion, they often employed children as lookouts or had them mark out the sites of recently buried corpses. Then these body snatchers could return at night and find the grave, without falling over a dozen headstones in the dark.

Peazle was quick to defend himself.

"You think it's easy for an orphan living in this city? I have to eat, you know." He angrily snatched the book from the larger boy. "I pick pockets too, I might as well tell you. It's either that or get sent up some chimney for a living, or maybe suffocate down a Lothian mine, opening trapdoors for the coal carts."

"Calm down, my friend." The highlander placed a hand on the smaller boy's shoulder. "I know what it's like tae go hungry myself. I was forced to come down from the highlands because there's nae work to be had in the north."

He spat on the ground in anger.

"I've been here over a week and I must admit I'm faring no better."

"No luck?"

"Oh, I have a job in an iron foundry where I work fae six in the morning till eight at night, for a few pennies. I sleep in a doorway because there are nae lodgings tae be had."

The pickpocket could see that Duncan's piercing blue eyes were ringed by dark circles and his fine cheekbones were made even sharper by exhaustion. It suddenly occurred to Peazle that his new friend wasn't nearly as old as he first appeared. He might only be a couple of years older than the pickpocket himself, perhaps fourteen or fifteen.

"I like it here because it's the only place in this overcrowded hellhole of a city where I can get a wee bit of peace." The highlander looked around at the laden boughs and lush green grass.

Peazle could see what he meant. Though dirty tenements surrounded the high walls of Greyfriars, the graveyard held only the funeral party, a courting couple and a few disrespectful urchins playing hide and seek. Tranquillity like that was rare in overcrowded Edinburgh, for famine and unsympathetic landowners had forced wave after wave of immigrants from the Scottish and Irish countryside to move to the cities. The population of the Old Town had doubled in the last thirty years.

"I spotted a hawk here yesterday," Duncan said. "A white one wi black tips on each wing. Ne'er seen anything like it before. Didnae look right in such a dirty sky."

The highlander grabbed a falling blossom and sniffed at it, but no fragrance could block out the smell of coal smoke and sewage that permeated the city.

"I come here a lot myself," the pickpocket replied. "Not just to spy on funerals," he added quickly. "I always sit here, on the grave of James Hogg."

He patted the stone on which he had been resting.

"He was a great poet, you know, and a man of learning. Yet he started as a humble shepherd, so I heard."

"Nothing wrong wi being a shepherd," Duncan scowled. "It was mah faither's profession."

"Listen, you helped me," the pickpocket said. "I'd like to return the favour. If you've nowhere to stay, you're welcome to lodge with me for a while."

Duncan thought for a second, then leaned behind a gravestone and picked up a small knapsack.

"Your hospitality is worthy of a highlander himself and I gladly accept. Where do you stay?"

"The Underground City."

"That sounds powerful grim."

"So does sleeping in a doorway. C'mon."

He led Duncan out of the graveyard, up the Old Town ridge and onto the High Street. For a few minutes, they pushed their way through the crowds thronging between the bristling tenements, until Peazle turned down a narrow and steeply sloping alley.

"The South Bridge," said Peazle as they neared the bottom. "Home sweet home."

The boys stood in the shadow of the bridge's towering pillars, its grimy brick flanks studded with openings leading to internal vaults. Chambers which had been designed to hold goods and wares, because of

Edinburgh's horrific overcrowding, now held people. The tenements that would eventually hide the vault entrances had not yet been built and Peazle and the highlander simply stepped from the street into the interior of the bridge. They made their way through a series of dark chambers and narrow passages, lit by dirty spluttering candles. After a while, their eyes grew accustomed to the murky light and the boys could make out vagabonds and beggars huddled in the darkened corners.

"This is my present place of residence." Peazle stepped into a smoky chamber, where three men were playing cards by candlelight. "It's smelly and dark and you might get murdered in your bed, but at least it's dry."

There was a squelch as he stepped through the doorway.

"Well, dry-ish."

"It smells tae high heaven." The highlander wrinkled his nose. "You actually pay for this?"

"I pay Merry Andrew." Peazle lowered his voice and indicated one of the card players, who slowly rose to his feet. Once he was standing, he had to stoop to avoid hitting his head on the roof. "He's the biggest, so the vault belongs to him."

The pickpocket waved to the rough-looking man. His face was a rash of pock marks and grey stubble, except for where a large scar ran from ear to chin.

"Merry. This is Duncan MacPhail from the high-lands. I want to share my space with him for a while."

Merry Andrew was far from merry. He looked like he could tear most men apart with his bare hands and was in the mood to do it.

"Oh really?" he growled, his voice broken by a lifetime of loud cursing and cheap grog. "Suppose I don't want Duncan MacPhail in my hoose? You think this place isn't crowded enough?"

He towered over the two boys.

"I reckon I'll throw Duncan out of my vault and charge you double for even suggesting it."

"Then Duncan might come back in the middle of the night and cut off your ears while you sleep." The highlander spoke softly but the small knife glinted in his hand once more. "If you're going tae make enemies so easily, it's better tae keep them close so you can see what they're up tae."

There was a stunned silence. The other card players looked at each other and gave a low whistle. Merry Andrew glowered. Then he half-smiled. Finally, he laughed out loud.

"Well spoken, boy." He slapped Duncan on the back. "I like your spirit. Ha'penny a week and you can stay. I collect the money prompt each Friday."

Peazle finally let his breath out.

Later that night, Merry Andrew and his companions went to the local tavern to play dice. The highlander and the pickpocket sat talking in the candlelight.

"Where did you get such a fine book?" Duncan picked up Peazle's journal. "It looks expensive. I see you've a fine quill pen too."

"Stole them from one of the bookstalls in Blair Street," the pickpocket admitted. "I always wanted to write something of value, as men of learning do. Taught myself to read in the poorhouse, I did.."

"I cannae read nor write myself," the highlander replied. "Where I come from, it was more important to learn how tae hunt and fight." He lay down on the pile of rough sacks and straw that served as bedding in the Underground City. "Still… it seems a shame to waste such a bonny volume."

"What do you mean?"

"Why don't you stop using it to dae the body snatchers dirty work? Keep a proper diary instead." The highlander blew out the candle, plunging the vault into darkness. "Someone might want tae read it years from now. Then you'll live forever."

"I doubt that," said the pickpocket. But he lay awake for a long time, smiling in the dark.

He had a proper friend at last and, to show his gratitude, he vowed to take Duncan's advice.

The Giant

Next morning, Charlie burst into the big top in a state of high excitement. Lilly was balancing three chairs, one on top of the other, at the end of her chin.

"I read the diary! Last night! Well, some of it. It was amazing… just like I was there. In fact, I don't even know if I dreamed it…"

He stopped in mid-tirade.

"Isn't that a bit heavy?"

"Itsh jusht an illushion," Lilly said without taking her eyes off the chairs. "You sheem very animated thish morning."

"It's this diary. It was written by a boy called Peazle, a real boy from two hundred years ago! He had a best friend, Duncan, who came down from the highlands to look for work in Edinburgh." Charlie spread his arms, trying to convey the enormity of what he was saying. "It was like I was *seeing* what went on."

"Musht be a quite a book."

"You don't understand. I can't explain it but somehow… I'm not just reading it. The book has only sketchy details and I only read a couple of pages, but I still know what went on in their lives. Stuff that's not even written down."

Charlie pulled the diary from his rucksack.

"Listen. I have to go to Greyfriars Graveyard."

Lilly jerked her head back and the chairs collapsed in perfect formation, stacking neatly as they landed. Charlie blinked.

"Why Greyfriars Graveyard?" she said sharply.

"Eh? I want to see where Peazle liked to hang out. He used to write on the grave of some guy called James Hogg. Duncan liked it too because it had hawks, just like the highlands."

"Hawks?" Lilly scowled.

"Well, one hawk. White with black-tipped wings." Charlie held up the book. "You want to come?"

"No, I don't." The girl turned sharply away. "I have to practise."

"Are you OK?" Charlie said, but Lilly ignored him and began to juggle again - seven balls, then eight, then ten, so fast they were merely a blur. When she did not turn around as he left, Charlie got the strangest feeling the girl was upset and trying to hide it.

Greyfriars was only a few hundred yards from the Old Town, but you could walk straight past without knowing it, for the cemetery was hidden by a high wall and ringed by old buildings. Charlie was lucky to spot the entrance, set back from the street between a pub and a row of small shops.

He let out a gasp as he walked through the wrought-iron gates. Dotted between the trees were carved gravestones, now weathered with age. Behind that was a high backdrop of grey Victorian tenements, exactly as he had pictured them the night before. The boy strolled round the side of the squat, barn-like church that faced the gates. There was the flat tombstone that marked the final resting place of James Hogg, right where he knew it would be.

"This is more than a little weird," Charlie muttered to himself, taking the journal from his bag. The worn stone was warm from the summer sun and, on impulse, he lay down on it, looking around to see if anyone disapproved. But the graveyard, hidden behind its double barricade, seemed to be deserted - so Charlie opened the book and began to read.

Sunday is the only day when Duncan duz not wurk at the factory and so we arranged to mete on the High Street in the afternoon, for in the morning he was paying his respects to a Gypsy girl who sings for mony in Blair Street and with whom he is much taken. I was in powerful good spirits for I had releeved more than one rich merchant of his gold snufbox that week...

Peazle walked slowly down the High Street, looking out for Duncan. Like all thoroughfares in the Old Town, the High Street was packed with people shopping and gossiping and it smelled strongly of sewage, for the ground was not paved and waste and rubbish was often thrown out of the windows at night. The air was filled with the shouts of fruit sellers and fishwives plying their wares from rickety wooden stalls planted in the stagnant mud. He finally found Duncan sitting on a stone stoop and looking glum.

"I presume things did not go entirely well with your girl this morning?" Peazle hunkered down beside his friend and tried to look sympathetic.

"She's no my girl, merely a pretty lassie who's company I like." Duncan poked dejectedly in the mud with his foot. "I'm fond of her and she can sing love ballads fit tae break a heart, but I'm a plain-spoken lad and no much for romantic talk."

"Well, don't ask me for advice. I'm too scrawny for courting. You fancy a bag of buckies?"

Peazle pointed to a stall selling little saucers of mussels, covered in salt and pepper.

"I dinnae want to eat anything that looks like it came out of someone's nose," the highlander grunted.

Peazle bought a saucer anyway. He had taken to hanging around Edinburgh's bookstalls to hear what the learned gentlemen who browsed there were saying. Usually, he couldn't comprehend much of their sophisticated talk but would grab a silk handkerchief or gold coin from their back pockets as they strolled past. Last week the pickpocket had overheard one gent say that eating fish made people smarter and decided seafood was his best bet for getting an education. Since mussels were the only kind of marine life he could actually afford, Peazle had taken to scoffing them whenever he got the chance.

The two boys sat on the cracked step while Peazle shovelled cold, slimy shellfish into his mouth and Duncan glowered at the thronging crowds. The highlander badly missed the solitude of his heather covered moors. Here he could see only slivers of sky between the tenement blocks and even those thin patches were tainted by thick palls of chimney smoke.

Duncan would have liked to get out of the grimy, overcrowded city for the day, but Peazle insisted he was scared of the countryside. The pickpocket had lived most of his life in slums and wasn't about to venture into a wilderness, where they might both get eaten by a wild animal. Especially a camel. Peazle was deathly afraid of camels after he had heard a learned gentleman say how bad-tempered they were.

"There's nae camels in the Scottish countryside," Duncan muttered. "I'm sure of it."

"Have you ever seen one?" Peazle asked.

"I dinnae even ken what a camel is."

"There you go, then," Peazle said triumphantly. "The countryside could be full of man-eating camels and you wouldn't know it."

Duncan wasn't giving up.

"We could go and climb up Arthur's Seat." The highlander pointed south to where a craggy hilltop could be glimpsed through the swirling smoke and chimney pots. "That's no exactly the countryside now, is it? You can see it from here."

Peazle looked at his friend in horror.

"You must be joking! When that thing blows up, I don't want to be standing on top of it."

Idling outside his favourite bookstall the week before, Peazle had been perturbed to hear two academics talking about Arthur's Seat being an extinct volcano with a vast network of tunnels underneath. Once he had asked around and found out what a volcano was, Peazle vowed never to set foot on the hill again. He was still trying to find out what extinct meant.

He half-heartedly offered the highlander a mussel but Duncan waved it away with a snort. Peazle could see his friend was in a foul mood but wasn't about to go climbing over a volcano just to cheer him up.

Duncan sighed loudly.

"Tell you what," the pickpocket said finally. "I'll buy us some decent food for tonight, eh? I've had a good week and it's time to sell what I've… eh… acquired."

He wiped greasy hands down his trousers and inspected his nimble fingers with pride.

"It means we'll have to go back to the Underground City for a bit, if you don't mind."

"If I'm getting something other than boiled turnip for supper, I'm willing tae trek through the very gates of hell."

"Funny you should say that," Peazle grinned uncomfortably as he stood. "C'mon, let's get this over with."

Duncan's mood was black as they marched back to the shadows of the South Bridge, stepped out of the sunlight and entered the familiar dark corridor that led to their vault. This time, however, the boys continued past the rude dwelling and carried on down the passageway. The highlander had never been in this direction before. He spent as much time as he could on the surface and was not inclined to delve deeper into the black, smelly corridors.

"Never thought we'd end up back in here on my day off," he muttered, tripping over a sleeping figure curled up on the tunnel floor. The passages, like every other part of Edinburgh, were festooned with down and outs who slept when they felt like it. And why not? In the permanent darkness of the Underground City, it was always night.

"Here we are," Peazle whispered finally, crouching beside a damp wall. "There's a set of stairs behind a little opening down here. Most people don't even know it exists."

His hunched form moved forward and, without warning, he was gone.

Puzzled, Duncan shuffled one near-invisible foot around in front of him where the wall met the floor and felt a small opening – he could have passed it a hundred times in the blackness without realising it was there. He sat down, wriggled his body through the gap and, leaning carefully on the slimy wall, inched slowly down a hidden stairway, feeling for each new step with his foot.

There was another tunnel at the bottom of the stairway and it seemed even darker than the one he had left, though Duncan didn't suppose this was actually possible. He heard a scratching noise to his right and Peazle's triumphant expression was lit by a crackling flame.

"Torches," the pickpocket said proudly, waving a stout stick that dripped flaming tar in alarming amounts. "Made em myself. You never know when the Old Town Guard will raid the place and I might have to make a quick getaway."

Duncan sighed. Edinburgh's Old Town Guard were mostly ex-soldiers well over retirement age. It was unlikely that they would bother raiding a den of vice-like the Underground City and weren't likely to catch more than a cold if they did.

In the light of the firebrand, the highlander could see this stonework was much older and cruder than the tunnels above and the walls shone with waterlogged moss. The smell was different too, not the stink of stale sweat and smoke that filled most of the chambers, but a wet, earthy smell that reminded Duncan of the caves under highland waterfalls. Peazle moved away again and he followed, touching the walls and sniffing his fingers.

"This is no bad, actually!" he grinned. "Peaceful, ye ken? I cannae hear anyone. Why does nobody live down here?"

"It's too damp and cold, even for beggars and drunks," Peazle said. "As far as I know, there's only one person staying on this whole level and that's who we're going to see."

"Who might *he* be?"

"His name's Shadowjack Henry, a blacksmith by trade. He moved down here a couple of months ago. There's a well at the end of this level that's been blocked up for as long as anyone can remember, so Shadowjack set up a wee forge and opened the well to draw water. He makes metal trinkets and sells them to the market traders on the High Street. The forge makes the vault warm enough to live in and there's no one else down here to pay rent to. A nice wee set-up, if you ask me."

"Sounds like it," Duncan agreed. "How is it I've never heard anyone mention him before?"

"You know how superstitious ignorant people are," Peazle said, as if he had the benefit of a fancy education. "There's some old legend about the well being haunted," he continued with a laugh. "Something about it leading straight down to hell."

Duncan stopped.

"Let's go back."

Peazle turned in astonishment. "Eh? What's the matter?"

"I'm not going intae any haunted place," Duncan said matter-of-factly.

"What?" Peazle spluttered, "I thought highlanders weren't scared of man nor beast! At least that's what you keep telling me about fifty times a day."

"Haunted stuff isnae man nor beast." Duncan shook his head. "Haunted stuff is witches and Kelpies and the Little People. In the highlands, you dinnae mess wi creatures like that, especially the Little People."

He folded his arms in determination.

"I cannae believe that you of all people would come down here, you that's scared of anything that moves."

"I'm scared of camels and volcanoes but that's scientific stuff," Peazle explained. "This is the 19th Century, Duncan. There's no such thing as Little People. Most of the trouble we get is from big people."

Duncan shook his head in exasperation but he was fiercely loyal to his friend and, after a stream of disapproving grunts, finally indicated to keep going.

For a while, the two boys walked without talking, the only sound being Peazle's tatty old boots crunching on loose stones and the rasp of his breathing. The pickpocket had to keep stopping to catch his breath. A lifetime of sleeping in the Underground City and a diet of turnip and salted beef hadn't done much for his health. Duncan didn't try to hurry him, for the wiry highlander was concerned about his frail friend and wasn't all that keen to get to where he was leading, anyway. Unlike Peazle, Duncan moved silently, as he had learned to do while stalking deer. Only now he walked without a sound in case something was creeping up on *him*.

Eventually, a flickering glow appeared at the far end of the tunnel and they could hear a muffled clanging, like a bell, growing louder as they walked. Peazle stopped and gave a long whistle.

The ringing stopped. After a few seconds, they heard a similar sound coming from the direction of the light, so Peazle signalled Duncan to carry on. At the end of the passageway, the boys turned a corner and a blast of hot, smoke-filled air seared their faces. They stepped from the dark passageway into a bright chamber and came upon a sight that would have confirmed the worst fears of the other underground dwellers.

Shadowjack Henry stood in the middle of the red, shimmering vault, stripped to the waist and swinging an enormous hammer. He was so large, he made Merry Andrew look like a midget and his massive torso, shining with exertion, bore the livid weals of a hundred healed burns. He brought the hammer down on the glowing metal rod he was shaping and a shower of dazzling sparks flew into the air, vanishing into the fierce radiance that emanated from the blacksmith's forge. Over the fire, a large metal smelting dish was suspended on a stout pole between two wooden tripods, powerful flames licking its sooty sides.

"My God," whispered Duncan. "We're in the doorway tae Hades itself."

Shadowjack looked round. Huge teeth split his bushy black beard as he grinned at the pickpocket.

"Peazle, my lad." He dropped the tool with a clang and raised a sweaty hand in greeting. The smile vanished as he caught sight of Duncan.

"Ah. I see you brought a visitor."

Shadowjack Henry flexed his considerable muscles and two bushy eyebrows closed ranks on his sweaty forehead.

"I don't get many visitors," he said coldly. "Being a private sort of person."

"This is Duncan MacPhail," the pickpocket gulped. "Don't worry, he's a good friend and one that I would trust with my life."

"That's the type of friend that you want, right enough." The giant smith looked the highlander up and down before turning back to Peazle.

"So, what have you brought for me, little man?"

The pickpocket pulled a canvas bag from under his shirt and emptied the contents onto the vault floor. Four snuffboxes glinted in the iridescent light. Shadowjack knelt and inspected them.

"Solid gold and good quality too. They'll make a pretty puddle once they're melted down. Well done, lad."

He went to a pile of bedding in the corner of the vault and rummaged inside.

"I'll give four shillings for the lot, as I'm in an uncommon generous mood."

The blacksmith smiled thinly and folded a few coins into Peazle's hand, his massive fingers enveloping the boys, like a shark swallowing a minnow. Shadowjack cast a sideways look at Duncan, to see if he had any opinion on the price, but the highlander was staring into the well. It looked harmless enough, just a round hole in the corner of the floor, with yet another wooden frame and pulley built over it. A rope and bucket sat nearby.

"Is this where you draw the water tae work your forge?"

"It is, boy." The blacksmith nodded. "And there are those who would like nothing better than for me to block that hole up again. Fortunately, I'm far too big to argue with."

He motioned with his hand.

"Don't fall in, though, for I won't venture down to rescue you."

"Don't worry, we're just going." Peazle was wafting the air in vain, his face already running with perspiration. "Let's get out of here, Duncan, before I faint dead away with the heat."

The highlander was still trying to peer into the darkness of the well, so Peazle grasped his arm and ushered him quickly out of the vault. Shadowjack didn't bother to say goodbye.

"He doesn't much like others' company, especially strangers," the pickpocket explained, as the scarlet glow faded behind them. "But I told you we'd eat well tonight."

He showed Duncan the pile of shillings.

"That well, back there?" his friend paused. "You can hear water running at the bottom."

"So what?"

"Water in a well doesnae run anywhere. What I heard was a stream."

"And that means?" Peazle looked none the wiser.

"I thought you were the scientific one," the highlander scoffed. "It means the water down there is coming from somewhere and going somewhere,"

He patted Peazle on the shoulder.

"It means there's another level underneath this one."

Charlie sat up with a start, not sure if he had been dreaming or simply lost in his own thoughts. The sun had gone behind a cloud and James Hogg's tombstone, wrapped in afternoon shadows, was cold against his skin. He sat up quickly and closed the journal.

Charlie knew exactly where Shadowjack Henry had once worked. He had been in that very chamber the day before and seen the remains of the blacksmith's forge - he recalled the discarded tripod and stone circle. The pile of rocks he had removed must have been covering up the well. Sealed by some kind of iron plug - and just as well, for hadn't the terrifying drumming noise come from somewhere under it? Charlie shivered again and the sensation hadn't much to do with the temperature this time.

All the same, he looked up to see where the sun had gone and his shiver turned into a gasp.

Floating, far above his head, was a white hawk with black-tipped wings.

The Dungeons

Charlie returned to the guesthouse, his mind whirling. Like the last time he had opened Peazle's diary, the boy was not sure if he had imagined or actually witnessed the events in the past. But there was no doubt that he had actually seen a hawk, right here and now, identical to the one Duncan described two centuries ago. Perhaps the bird's descendants still nested in the area and, by some genetic fluke, bore the same markings. Then again, maybe all the hawks round here were white with black-tipped wings – Duncan didn't seem to know much about the lowland wildlife of Scotland and neither did Charlie.

Anyway, the boy had more pressing questions. How had Shadowjack Henry's well come to be blocked up - hidden under a pile of rocks along with Peazle's book? What was the mysterious rapping he had heard in the Underground City? And what exactly happened to the boys from the past?

By the time Charlie reached the guesthouse, his parents had left for their nightly performance at the big top. A little tray of biscuits and tea-bags were provided in each room, so the boy grabbed a handful of chocolate digestives, opened the journal, and lay down on the bed to read.

The next Sunday we arranged to mete in the afternoon once more, as Duncan had gone calling on his lady friend again and he seems to be creeture of habit. I was bored wating and knowing that the castle esplanade was filed with gentlemen taking the air, I vowed to liten a few of their back pokets before returning to find my frend...

Edinburgh Castle was on the highest pinnacle of the Old Town ridge. The muddy road that led to it was steep and slippery and Peazle was wheezing like a donkey long before he reached the top. Eventually, the slope opened onto the castle esplanade, an exposed area leading to the huge iron portcullis that fronted the massive fortress walls. Since the other three sides of the castle overlooked sheer cliff faces, the esplanade was the only real way to reach the castle - which left potential invaders horribly exposed. It was said that the approach was exactly the length an arrow could be accurately fired.

In peacetime, however, the esplanade's tremendous height made it the perfect spot for sightseeing. The area was filled with young men trying to impress lady friends by wearing their Sunday best and pretending to know the names of far off hills. Peazle strolled around like the city's scruffiest tourist, secretly eyeing them buying cups of flavoured ice for their paramours and watching where they kept their purses.

"A fool and his money are soon parted, and love makes a fool of the wisest man," the pickpocket said sagely. "Ooh. I must write that down."

While Peazle was spying on potential victims, Duncan sat at the bottom of Blair Street, listening to the Gypsy girl as she sang to the crowds. Like so many of the Old Town's narrow wynds, Blair Street sloped steeply down from the High Street until it vanished into the slums of the Cowgate. Each wynd had its own distinct character and this particular thoroughfare was lined with bookstalls and filled with what Peazle always referred to as 'learned gents', browsing idly among leather-bound volumes. Near the bottom of the street, the stalls thinned out and passers-by often paused to listen to the girl, for she had a voice that made words sweeter than any book. She and the highlander had struck up a friendship and he visited often.

This time, however, her tune was making Duncan melancholy – a lament about clans forced to leave their homeland after the doomed highland revolt of 1745. Even the girl's name reminded him of the highlands.

Heather.

Halfway through her refrain, Heather noticed Duncan's expression and broke off in mid-tune. She picked up a few grubby coins and, to the disappointment of the gathered crowd, came and sat beside him. Thick black hair swung across a radiant face as she lowered herself down.

"Is my singing making you sad?" She looked sideways at him.

"The song is," he replied. "All the more for being sung so beautifully."

"If you miss the highlands so much, why did you leave?" Heather asked. "If I might be so bold," she added quickly - for she knew the highlander wasn't one to casually reveal his feelings.

But Duncan answered without any prompting, for the song had also reminded him of a great unfairness, and he felt injustices should always be brought into the open.

"The land my clan worked for generations was taken from them, so the laird could use it for his sheep to graze," he said, with undisguised disgust. "There was nae work anymore for the men who lived there."

"I'm sorry," Heather said. But Duncan hadn't finished.

"An outbreak of cholera five years ago killed many, my own faither included. The rest of my family booked passage for North Carolina, tae start a new life in the Americas."

The highlander's face was expressionless.

"My mother wouldnae go."

"Why not?"

There was a long silence before the boy spoke again.

"I had a brother, little more than an infant. Ma used to leave him in the doorway of oor croft, wrapped in a wee tartan shawl, while she picked wild berries. I was supposed tae be watching him. I looked away for only a few seconds, I swear."

He kept his head bowed but the Gypsy could hear pain cracking his voice.

"When I turned back, he was gone."

Heather covered her mouth with a dainty hand.

"I thought it must be a wolf or a starving dog that took him and searched the moorland for days. It was nae use." Duncan's voice had suddenly grown hard and flat. "Ma would not accept that. She said my brother had been taken by the Little People."

"The faerie folk?" Lilly nodded, unsurprised. In those days, people still believed in such creatures.

"Aye. My mother died of the cholera some months after but, until that time, she stood in the doorway every day at dusk and called my brother's name. Hoping the Little People might take pity and bring him back."

He looked up and smiled forlornly.

"They never did."

Pretending to stare at the view, Peazle stretched out his hand and slowly lifted the tailcoat of a young man who was chatting animatedly to his lady. A stiff breeze blew from the Pentland Hills across the esplanade and tore at the youth's clothes, making the pickpocket's practised manoeuvre impossible to detect. The wallet slid out of the back pocket, vanished into Peazle's vest and he gave a satisfied smile – the victim was so engrossed in his beau that the boy could have stolen his underwear.

As he turned to escape, the grin froze on his lips.

Two kilted soldiers stood behind him, pointing bayonets at his stomach.

Heather sat silently beside Duncan and, for a while, allowed the highlander his own thoughts. Eventually, she spoke again.

"Do *you* think the Little People took your brother?"

"I dinnae ken." The boy sighed. "At our clan gatherings, the old men used tae scare us with stories about them."

"It was the same with us Gypsies," Heather agreed. "According to our elders, the Little People have many names – Brownies, Elves, Faeries, Sprites, Imps and Pixies. Our legends say they used to live all over the world. But men began to spread across the globe and the Little People returned to their homeland of Galhadria."

The girl lowered her voice, as if some unseen being might be listening.

"They say that, in the quiet places of the earth, the Galhadrians sometimes return to dance or hunt - and it is a great misfortune for any man to come upon them."

Duncan was familiar with this part of the story. Children in the highlands had long been warned of 'thin places' - remote valleys and hilltops where the barrier between this world and the domain of the Little People were closest – though he had never heard the name Galhadria before. In these thin places, you might accidentally stumble on them dancing in the moonlight and, if you did, they would take you to their world. It wasn't that the Little People were evil, the old ones of the clan said. It was just that the wishes of men didn't mean much to them. Duncan supposed that was why they could steal a human baby without worrying what it might do to a mother or brother.

"We were told faeries sometimes take our children and leave one of their own in its place," he said. "And you cannae tell it's really one of the faerie folk until it grows up. Or sometimes they leave a horrible, deformed changeling. Or they dinnae leave anything at all. I wish I knew what was true."

He glanced round at Heather. The Gypsy girl was looking at the ground, her fists clenched.

"What's the matter, lass?"

"Nothing," she answered quietly. "I just think that legends can get mixed up over time. Even a small mix-up can change the meaning of everything, you know?"

Heather paused, as if she had more to say but, before Duncan could press her, she scrambled to her feet.

"I'd better give them another song. Something more cheerful."

She smiled and nodded towards another group of wealthy gents, milling beside the nearest bookstall. She began to sing again and the men gathered round and reached into their pockets.

Peazle had never been inside the castle before and, though he was truly impressed by the lofty battlements and smoke-blackened towers, he wished he could be anywhere else on the planet. The two soldiers marched him up the winding cobbled road into the very heart of the fortifications, past endless stone barracks, cannons and cooking fires. The castle hadn't seen conflict for half a century but it was still a military garrison. Kilted recruits and officers in bright tartan trews and scarlet jackets stared as the pickpocket was escorted past. The air pulsed with the smell of roasting meat and the sound of shouted orders.

"What are you going to do with me?" he asked one of the soldiers timidly.

"If it were oop ter me, lad, oi'd probably joost shoot yer," the man replied in a thick Irish brogue. "Boot it's ter the doonguns oim taking yer."

"The dungeons!" Peazle squealed, then quickly regained his composure. Panicking wasn't going to help this situation. "I thought they were only for prisoners of war."

"Dat dey is," the soldier replied. "Boot we're not at war with anyone at present and, as it happens, there's a coople o men down dere from the town council. I reckon oil joost hand yis over to them."

He motioned with his bayonet towards an oak doorway set in a tower wall and the other soldier pushed Peazle through. Behind the door, a steep staircase wound into the bowels of the castle and the soldiers' tackety boots clattered on the stone as they followed Peazle round and round and down and down, past cold gaping chambers fortified with iron bars. In the darkness of some of the vaults, Peazle could hear murmuring in some language he didn't understand.

"Dootch smooglers," said the talkative Irishman. "Oi can't oondershtand a bloody werd they're saying."

The trio eventually arrived at a long corridor lit by thick, acrid candles. A group of men, two soldiers and two civilians, were clustered around a table cluttered with paper, trying to read in the flickering light.

"Sah! The tunnel don't show up on any of the charts we have!" a sergeant with a giant walrus moustache barked. The civilians gave a little jump. "There's no telling where it might lead. Might be a few feet or…"

"…Or it might lead right under our defences." His companion, an officer of some sort, folded hands behind his back. "We simply have to find out where it goes. Can't fit any of our men in there, you say?"

"No, Sah!" The civilians winced again. "Not even Private Hemmingway, an he lost his legs at Waterloo." The sergeant thought for a second before adding, "And an arm."

The sergeant turned to Peazle and his guards.

"What might you be doing with that boy, private MacSorry?"

"Caught him stealing, Sor. Wallets. Oop on the esplanade."

"That's not a military matter," the officer reprimanded.

"I know Sor and I tot, since dere were two members of the town council here, oid bring him to dem."

The councillors, dressed in identical breeches and frock coats, looked up from their charts.

"It's not our concern, soldier," one said. "Deliver him to the town guard. He'll most likely be tried by the magistrate on Monday."

The officer stroked his broad chin thoughtfully before speaking.

"What will happen to the boy?"

"It's a serious charge, pick-pocketing, if he was caught red-handed." The councillors went back to studying their charts. "He'll be deported to a penal colony in Australia, like as not."

"Actually, I was just testing these fine soldiers' powers of observation." Peazle raised his hand. "And very alert they were too. I was going to put the money back…."

"Don't even bother, lad." The officer crouched down beside Peazle and put a hand on his shoulder. "But there might be a way we could forget this whole ehm… incident."

"Oh, I don't think that's possible." One councillor glanced up again. "Boy broke the law."

"What I'm proposing." The officer ignored the interruption. "Is for you to redeem yourself by a bit of bravery. Like a little soldier, eh?"

Peazle nodded enthusiastically, not having a clue what the officer was talking about. Encouraged, the man continued.

"We've found a tunnel in the dungeons, lad, and we didn't even know it was there. We have to figure out where it goes - but it's too small for any of my men to fit in, see?"

Peazle nodded again, more slowly this time. He was beginning to understand what the man was getting at.

"So if you was to have a little explore of this tunnel and tell us where it went, the army would consider this an act of patriotism, a great civic duty. Isn't that right, gentlemen?"

The councillors were nodding as well. Private MacSorry gave Peazle a thumbs-up sign.

"True. A boy would be forgiven a bit of thievery if he was as patriotic as that," one councillor said slyly. "Wouldn't get sent to Australia, neither."

Peazle looked from one looming adult to another. They leaned towards him, moustaches bristling.

"All right," said the pickpocket wearily. "Show me the tunnel."

"Wait a moment. How will we know where he's gone?"

"Drum, Sah!" screamed the sergeant and the councillors jumped once more. "There's a tiny drum in the officers' mess. It was made for Colonel Grouper's little boy, before he blew his head off playing with a loaded musket!"

"Excellent, sergeant. Fetch the drum and a firebrand for the lad." The officer leaned further towards Peazle.

"We're going to make a hero of you son, rather than a villain," he whispered, not unkindly.

Charlie sat up in bed, covered in sweat. He was still fully dressed but his mother must have removed his shoes and put a cover over him when she came home. The curtains were open and he could see the moon shining behind the spires of Edinburgh.

"My God… the legend," he whispered to himself, remembering the rapping he had heard in the Underground City.

"*Peazle's* the little drummer boy."

The Descent

Charlie felt as if he had slept most of the day and night. Perhaps he had, for now he was wide awake, itching to get up and do something. He put on his shoes, stuffed the diary inside his shirt and went to the window. The Old Town was hunched in the middle of Edinburgh like a sleeping dragon, a heavy moon gilding its jagged outline.

Charlie looked at his watch. It was five-thirty in the morning. He unlatched the window and stuck his head out. There was a drainpipe a couple of feet to the left, but his room was on the second floor and it was too dark to tell whether the garden below was grass, soil or paving. Yet suddenly, he wanted to know. In fact, he wanted to know everything. And not just know everything but to feel everything too – that was the closest he could come to describing it. For the first time, Charlie Wilson really wanted to be part of the adventure, rather than a spectator.

Almost without thinking, he pulled himself onto the broad window ledge and twisted round to grasp the drainpipe in both hands. He had never actually watched his parents perform the high wire act but had seen them

practise many times. And he recalled his father's favourite phrase.

Hesitation is an acrobat's worst enemy.

With a deep breath, Charlie swung one foot over the
pipe and planted it against the wall. He took his other
foot off the sill and began to climb down, hand over
hand. A minute later, he was standing on the dewy
grass, not even out of breath.

"That was better than any video game," he said
brightly, letting himself out of the garden gate and
heading towards the Old Town. "What have I been
missing?"

Edinburgh Festival's events went on until around
one in the morning and the pubs closed even later. At
this hour, however, even the most hardened partygoers
had gone to bed. The streets were deserted.

Charlie made his way up the High Street and onto
the castle esplanade. Far below, the lights of Edinburgh
glittered like a swarm of fireflies, while the castle was
a soaring block of darkness, casting a net of shadows
over the esplanade and turning monuments and trees
into sinister blobs. The boy felt like he was standing on
another world.

Then the first rays of dawn began to filter through
the tall tenements of the Royal Mile, spotting the castle
ramparts with light and laying golden strips along the
concrete. They lit a low, bordering wall and Charlie
went and sat on the ground with his back against it. As
minutes ticked by, the castle slowly turned from black

to charcoal to grey and the boy could make out the true outline of statues, railings and ticket booths. Eventually, it was light enough to read and he opened Peazle's diary.

He had to know what happened next.

The tunel was at the bak of the darkest deepest dungon and there was hardly room for even a boy of my small size to fit inside. I held the firebrand in front of me with one hand and dragged the drum behind me on a lether strap tied to my waste. The oficer had instructed me to stop every few minutes or so and bang the drum as loudly as I cood, so that he could hear where I was going. This prooved to be more difficult than he imagined...

The firebrand sputtered badly and the narrowness of the tunnel deflected the heat back into Peazle's face. He was forced to hold the torch as far in front of him as he could and crawl using his free arm. The leather strap attached to the drum kept getting tangled in his legs and the only way he could make a noise was to stop crawling and kick at the drum's taut skin with his feet.

The councilmen and soldiers at the entrance to the tunnel waited until the erratic banging was so faint they could hardly hear it.

"Sergeant," the officer said finally. "Take your men and scour the main courtyard. See if they can pick up the noise there. Put some out on the esplanade too."

"Yes, Sah!" The sergeant stood to attention, then hesitated. "Beggin your pardon Sah, but that drum the lad's dragging behind him fills the entire tunnel. If it comes to a dead-end, how's he going to get back?"

"This is a military garrison." The officer gave the sergeant a withering look. "We can't just have tunnels running who knows where. We need to know where it goes."

He turned and walked away.

Wriggling along the tiny passageway, Peazle was soon close to exhaustion. The firebrand in front of him was burning precious oxygen, what little air he could suck into his straining lungs was hot and thin and his elbows and knees throbbed, where rough stone had torn away the skin. Worst of all, he was gripped by a rising panic that was becoming harder and harder to quell. He wanted to scream in rage and fear and thrash at the walls - but knew this would use up even more air. Instead, he forced himself to lie still until he felt a semblance of calm return. Then he began to crawl forward once more.

When the pickpocket had almost given up hope, the little passage began to widen. Soon Peazle could crawl on his hands and knees, then manage a crouching shuffle. Finally, he was able to stand. He put the torch on the ground, fastened the drum round his waist and untied the drumsticks strapped to his thigh.

On the esplanade, Private MacSorry sat on a low wall, rolling a cigarette.

"MacSorry!" roared the sergeant. "I know the boy's probably dead already, or his extremities are being eaten by rats, but that doesn't mean you can give up looking...." He stopped suddenly and held up a large, scarred hand. "What's that?"

"What's what, Sir?"

"Silence, you horrible little man!" the sergeant screamed. "How am I supposed to concentrate with you wittering on!"

He dropped to his knees and pressed a hairy ear to the ground.

"It's drumming, Private. That's what it is. Under the ground." He looked up, moustache quivering and beckoned to the officer. "Sah! Over here!"

Peazle marched along the tunnel, firebrand raised high. Occasionally he stopped and beat the drum for a few seconds, but not very often, for the sound was deafening in such an enclosed space. The boy was wary of making a loud noise at the best of times. Pickpockets, out of sheer habit, didn't like to attract unwanted attention. And who knew what lurked in these passageways? Worse still, the tunnel had begun to slope steeply down. Now, with every step, he was moving deeper into the bowels of the earth.

Then he came to a door.

It was ancient and thick, its misshapen oak timbers covered in dark mould. Peazle groaned in disbelief.

"What on God's green earth is this doing here? It must weigh a ton and I'll wager its hinges are rusted solid with age." He gave a half-hearted shove at the oak giant. "I bet Goliath himself couldn't shift it."

The door swung open without a sound and Peazle fell through into another passage. The barrier shut again and the pickpocket sprang to his feet, swiping wildly at the air with his drumsticks and screaming. But no hidden monster appeared and this tunnel looked the same as it did on the other side of the door. Regaining his composure, Peazle turned and inspected the barrier more closely. The torch lit up the hinges, ornate, finely crafted and looking like they had been made yesterday.

"No wonder they didn't rust." The pickpocket breathed. "If I'm not mistaken, they're solid silver and finer than any snuffbox I've ever seen."

He ran his torch excitedly over the rest of the door – and found its surface was pitted with metal studs, glowing with a lambent beauty. They, too, were silver. Peazle grabbed a narrow rock and tried with all his strength to prise one off. The stud stayed put.

"Bother!" The pickpocket finally gave up. "Don't suppose there's much chance of stumbling on a crowbar." He stepped back and studied the door with growing suspicion. "Why would anyone go to the trouble of building such an ornate barricade way down here then make it so easy to get through?"

His eyes widened.

"Unless it only opens from one side!"

The pickpocket launched himself at the barrier and pushed with all his might. It didn't budge. He tried pulling on the silver studs but his hands just slipped off.

"Blast, blast, blast!!!" he sobbed. He attacked the door again, though he knew it was useless. He gave the unyielding wood one last kick, picked up the firebrand and continued, still cursing, down the tunnel. The unpleasant surprises weren't over for, before long, the tunnel forked. Peazle stared at identical passageways.

"Ach, both of these probably lead to certain death, so it doesn't matter which one I take."

He shrugged and went left. After a while, the tunnel split again, and then again, so every few minutes he had to make a fresh choice. Peazle tried to pick the passages that didn't slope too much but each corridor twisted and turned and led inexorably downwards. Desperation eventually overcame fear and, as the boy marched, he began to beat the drum - berating himself with each stroke for agreeing to this insanity. He would probably keep descending until he died from thirst or reached Australia after all.

He turned a corner and stopped dead.

Once again, the passageway split in different directions but, this time, the left-hand passage opened into a large chamber. It seemed to have suffered a rock fall, for, on one side of the vault, boulders rose at a steep angle from floor to roof.

The pickpocket's mouth fell open and the drumsticks dropped from his hands. Scattered across the sloping hill of stones were a mass of breastplates and helmets – while swords, spears and arrows protruded between the larger rocks. They glowed coldly in the firebrand's light. Peazle could tell, at a glance, the weapons and armour, like the door studs, were made of solid silver.

The boy was looking at more wealth than he had ever imagined, and he could imagine a *lot* of wealth. He clambered onto the rockfall and ran trembling hands over the shining surfaces.

"This is the best thing that ever happened to me," he sighed, laying his cheek reverently on a gleaming breastplate. "Now I really do have to get out of here alive."

He cast an expert eye over the treasure until he spotted what he was sure was the finest piece. Near the ceiling, a beautifully engraved sword, complete with a jewel-encrusted handle, was wedged between boulders. The pickpocket scrambled to the top, grasped the handle and pulled with all his might. The sword gradually eased out of the narrow gap, remarkably light in his hand, smouldering with a steely blush that seemed to come from within.

"This will do nicely."

Peazle climbed back down the rock pile, the drum banging awkwardly against his knees. With a grunt, he unfastened a clasp on the leather strap and it crashed to the ground, then rolled off down the tunnel. Peazle fastened the sword in its place, picked up the firebrand and set off down the passage, whistling to himself. Now that he carried a weapon worth a fortune, the pickpocket was filled with a newfound enthusiasm.

Halfway down the Royal Mile, the sergeant took his ear from the ground and slowly stood up. On one side of his head, his hair, matted with mud, stuck out like a small explosion. The councillors and the officer looked at him expectantly.

"The drumming kept getting fainter, Sah, as if the boy was getting further and further underground." He took a deep breath. "Then it stopped."

There was silence for a few seconds before the officer turned to the councillors.

"That's not an escape tunnel - not if it goes down that far." He turned to the sergeant. "Order the men back to the dungeons and have them seal the passage up."

"Ehm. Begging pardon, Sah." The sergeant looked flustered, for he was not used to questioning his superiors. "Just because the drum stopped doesn't mean the boy is dead."

"No indeed, sergeant." The officer tapped an ivory-topped cane angrily against his leg. "But my priority is the defence of the castle, not the fate of some thief."

He turned his back, indicating their brief conversation was over.

"Yes, Sah." The sergeant motioned to MacSorry and his companions to follow and marched purposefully back up the High Street. He had seen children die before. The drummer boy of his own regiment had been swept away in a French cannon blast at the battle of Aurerstadt. He didn't approve, of course, but orders were orders.

Charlie opened his eyes. The whole of the esplanade was bathed in early morning sunlight and the brass statues lining the sides were shining like precious metal. He had long ago given up doubting what he was seeing was real. How that was possible was something he could ponder later.

"Breastplates and helmets and swords," the boy breathed softly. "All solid silver and encrusted with jewels."

He remembered Lilly's words when he had first shown her the note.

I bet it means there's treasure hidden down there...

"You said it, girl!" Charlie laughed, shutting the diary. Then the laugh died in his throat as he recalled what she had said next.

What if those council workers end up heading towards it?

Charlie sprang to his feet and raced down the High Street towards the big top.

The Forge

Charlie half expected to see Lilly juggling elephants or something equally bizarre when he burst into the theatre. Instead, she was sitting on the floor, in her usual green dress, drinking a can of coke.

The boy's face was red and sweating after running halfway down the Royal Mile, so Lilly held out the drink. He took a huge gulp and bubbles shot out of his nose.

"Charming."

"Listen!" The boy spluttered after three minutes of uncontrollable hiccupping. "There really is treasure in the Underground City. In a set of blocked up tunnels! It's in Peazle's journal. Ehm. Sorry."

He handed the can, overflowing with froth, back to Lilly. She looked at it in disgust.

"There's silver," Charlie continued. "Loads of it, according to this book."

"Told you." The girl allowed herself a triumphant smile.

"Yeah, but we're in trouble. Council workers will soon be excavating down there. You said so yourself." Charlie pointed to the back of the big top. "We need to get underground and find that treasure before they do."

"We? I thought I was just the lookout."

"I don't know about you," Charlie replied vehemently. "But that treasure would mean an awful lot to me. You've never seen where I live - it's small and cheap cause my parents hardly make any money. If you hadn't noticed, there isn't exactly a lot of work at the job centre for acrobats."

"Hey, hey." Lilly held up a hand. "Calm down and take a seat before you explode."

She pulled Charlie down beside her and he sat, chest heaving - trying to get his emotions, as well as his breathing, under control.

"For a start, you don't know if the council workers will end up anywhere near the treasure."

"They might," Charlie interrupted, running a hand through his hair. "All they have to do is break into the bottom tunnels."

"Calm down." Lilly took the boy's hand and stared earnestly into his face, her green eyes somehow soothing him. "Charlie, we don't even know if the treasure is still there."

The boy began to shake his head but she squeezed his hand tighter.

"The diary is almost two hundred years old, remember?"

He nodded sullenly.

"You need to read the rest of the book before you go rushing into the dark again." She gave one last squeeze before letting go. "Find out exactly what's down there."

"You're right." Charlie stood up and went to the ranks of chairs where the audience normally sat. He plonked himself down and pulled out the diary.

"What are you doing?"

"Taking your advice." He looked up. "I'm going to finish this. Go ahead and juggle if you want."

He bent over the book and began reading. Lilly pulled several multicoloured balls from her pockets and began to toss them in the air, her hands moving faster and faster, until the objects were no more than a whirling smear. After a while, the balls were joined by glittering stars, circling around each other like a tiny galaxy. One of the balls burst into flames without interrupting its mad spinning. Charlie didn't look up.

Lilly sighed. The balls began to vanish one by one. Their motions got slower and the stars glittered less brightly, then went out. Finally, only the flaming ball spun uncertainly on the end of the girl's finger. With a flick of her wrist, her hand enveloped the flame, snuffing it. The object dropped, smoking, to the floor.

Lilly walked over to Charlie.

"Budge up then," she said, sitting next to him. "Let's have a look."

The tunel seemed to be levelling out at last and I was no longer scared of meeting any monsters, or not very much. For I had my magnificent sword, which I intended to sell as soon as I cood find my way to the surface…

"Uh oh."

Peazle glanced up at his spluttering torch. The shadows in the tunnel were becoming thicker and darker, as the firebrand's flame grew lower. The pickpocket increased his pace but couldn't go much faster, for the extent of his ill health was making itself painfully obvious. The boy had a nagging stitch in his side, his breath was coming in broken gasps and the reduced light meant he stumbled on the uneven floor every few feet, sometimes sprawling headfirst across the pitted floor. On the fourth or fifth fall, he lay exhausted while the firebrand's flame faded to dirty red embers and the tunnel melted into terrifying blackness. Still lying on the floor, Peazle curled into a ball and began to cry.

Gradually, his sobbing turned to a shivering whimper, for the tunnel was cold and the heat Peazle had worked up during his earlier exertions was evaporating. He closed his eyes and pulled his elbows and knees in tighter, trying to shut out the cold, darkness and fear.

Lying perfectly still made him aware of something he hadn't noticed before. He could hear a faint, sinister hiss somewhere up ahead.

"Snake?"

Peazle's eyes shot open and one hand went instinctively to the hilt of his sword. He drew the weapon slowly from the leather belt and held it protectively in front of his face. To his astonishment, the sword glowed with a pale blue luminance, not as effective as the firebrand, but enough to let him see a few feet of the passage ahead. Peazle knew that lying doing nothing, no matter how scared he felt, wasn't going to solve his predicament – and *something* was making that hiss. It might be a giant underground snake, but it might also be a wind blowing in from somewhere outside.

There was only one way to find out, so he struggled to his feet and started forwards, jabbing the weapon aggressively before him. Whenever the tunnel branched, Peazle listened carefully, then went in the direction of the noise. He knew he was choosing well for, at each fork, the sound got louder - though never as loud as the pounding of his heart.

The passage ended and Peazle found himself looking into a smooth volcanic chamber, triangular in shape and not much higher than his head. At the narrow end, a stream emerged from one rock fissure and rolled sluggishly through a gash in the floor, eroded by centuries of flowing water. At the wider end, it vanished into the darkness again. Peazle gripped his sword handle tighter, for the surface of the steam danced and sparkled with a strange red light that made the water look suspiciously like blood. The pickpocket had once overheard a conversation between two learned gents about Greek mythology, whatever that was. They recounted a story of how dead souls were ferried down an underground river and into Hades, which was guarded by a three-headed hound called Cerberus.

"Nice doggy," The pickpocket sank to his knees, clasping both hands in front of his face. "Oh, God. Please, please, get me out of this."

He closed his eyes, praying to whatever deity happened to be listening.

"I've always wanted to die rich, but not ten minutes after I *got* rich." He opened one eye and looked pleadingly upwards. "C'mon, I'll do anything. Just give me a sign."

An object came hurtling out of the blackness above and plunged into the stream, showering the pickpocket with icy needles of water. He scuttled back against the chamber wall, gasping with cold and thrusting his sword ineffectively in the general direction of the unknown attacker. The water broke again and a wooden bucket, tied to the end of a rope, emerged full and dripping from the watercourse. It rose jerkily back up and vanished into a glowing red hole in the chamber roof.

"Woah! Hey! Whoever's up there!" the pickpocket screamed at the top of his voice. "I'm down here! Here! Oh damn!"

He still held the silver sword.

He looked round in panic and, spotting a large boulder, ran over and pushed the sword into the shadows and covered it with stones. He whirled back, took a deep breath, jumped into the icy stream and waded to the centre of the chamber. Above him, he could now see a long, thin funnel rising twenty feet through the solid rock of the chamber roof, ending in a circle of red light.

Suddenly he realised exactly where he was.

"Shadowjack! Shadowjack Henry! I'm down here!" the pickpocket yelled up the funnel. He waved his arms maniacally, though nobody above could possibly see him. "I'm at the bottom of your well!"

A bearded face appeared in the red circle, far above.

"Peazle? Is that you I can hear, lad?" Shadowjack's voice echoed down the shaft. "How the hell did you get down there?"

The rope and bucket came hurtling down again. Shivering and crying, Peazle sat on the bucket, arms and legs wrapped around the sodden rope and Shadowjack Henry pulled him to safety.

A few minutes later, Peazle was sitting in the blacksmith's vault, wrapped in a woollen blanket and sipping a cup of hot ale. A pot of the sweet-smelling brew bubbled on the forge and the pickpocket's clothes hung, steaming, on the bar above. Shadowjack sat next to the boy, stripped to the waist, holding his own mug in a giant scarred hand. He listened intently, occasionally nodding, while Peazle told him about his underground journey. The pickpocket missed out the part about the treasure, however. He wasn't about to trust such a big man with so much wealth at stake.

"That's a fine adventure, without a doubt," Shadowjack said, when Peazle had finished. The two stared at each other for a long time until the blacksmith spoke again.

"If you go back to the surface, they'll probably just arrest you."

Peazle nodded bitterly.

"No. I don't think I'd be much of a friend if I let you go back up top." Shadowjack stroked his beard slowly, still looking keenly at the boy. The pickpocket couldn't see much friendliness in that stare.

They sat in silence for a while longer, Shadowjack watching him intently. Finally, Peazle couldn't stand it anymore.

"You know about the treasure, don't you?" he said bluntly.

"Aye, I do," Shadowjack admitted. "You think anything but treasure would keep me in this hellhole? I've not seen a bloody tree in months."

The giant stretched a burly arm over the forge and shifted Peazle's clothes so they wouldn't scorch. He took another gulp of his ale.

"I was a fine smithy, you know," he said. "Used to work out by Kelty, across the River Forth. I did all right when we was fighting Napoleon and the army needed cannon and cartwheels and the like. But, after the war, many that harvested the land left for the cities - for they have machines now that can do their work."

Shadowjack spat on the floor to show what he thought of mechanised farming.

"Me? I couldn't labour in some hot, cramped factory."

Peazle looked incredulously around the sweltering little vault.

"How on earth did you end up down here?"

"I went to Leith docks to enlist in the King's Navy. I'd got to like quite like cannon and thought I might make a good cabin boy."

Peazle frowned. He could never tell if Shadowjack was joking or just slightly insane. The big man carried on with his tale of woe.

"I was having a last whisky or three in one of the taverns there, when I overheard two Gypsy types talking in a corner. A mite the worse for the grog they were, and a bit louder than they intended to be. I only caught the end of what they were saying, but it sounded powerful interesting to me. Another ale?"

"No thanks."

Shadowjack poured more steaming liquid into the boy's cup anyway.

"One was telling the other some old Gypsy legend, about how there was supposed to be untold riches, hidden in a well under Edinburgh." Shadowjack took another large swig of his brew. The fact that it was still boiling didn't seem to bother him.

"Anyway, I'd heard from a beggar that there happened to be a blocked up well at the bottom of the Underground City."

"So you decided to abandon a life on the ocean wave and move here?" Peazle looked sceptical.

"To be honest, I can't swim." The big blacksmith grinned. "Besides, the only ship in port was a barge carrying treacle to Glasgow. So I came down here, built a forge and opened up the well." He pointed to the forbidding hole in the corner of the vault. "Late at night, I'd climb down the shaft and search for the treasure. Took me a while to find it, though not as fast as you, eh?"

"Yes. I was born lucky." Peazle snorted. "So, how are you going to spirit all that silver away without anyone spotting it?"

"Simple. I'm melting it down in the forge."

"You're what!"

Instead of replying, Shadowjack padded over to the farthest corner of the vault and picked up a large knife. Peazle clutched his mug tighter. The blacksmith pulled a horseshoe from his pocket, scraped at it with his blade and held it out. Under the dirty iron surface, the metal gleamed brightly.

Peazle drew in breath sharply.

"Throw on a bit of dirt when it's hot and a silver horseshoe will look as drab and worthless as any iron one. When I've turned all the spoils into these horseshoes, I'll pile them on a cart and ride out of Edinburgh a rich man." He grinned slyly. "Your outfit's dry."

Warily, Peazle took the stiff, warm clothes and put them on, while Shadowjack stood up and stretched. The movement put him between the pickpocket and the vault door. His shadow rose menacingly up the wall and flickered across the roof.

He was still holding the knife, its surface reflecting the blood-red glow of the fire.

"However, if anyone informed on me?" He looked darkly at the boy, and Peazle shrank back from the bushy gaze. "I'd find myself fighting off every thief and vagabond in the city."

"I wouldn't tell," Peazle said in a small voice. "Not ever."

"I want to believe that, lad." Shadowjack took a step forward. Peazle saw the giant was perspiring more than he ever had working on his forge. "I like you, boy, but that's an awful chance to take."

Peazle began to back away as Shadowjack advanced. His mind was working furiously.

"There is an *awful* lot of silver. Enough to make more than one person rich." He saw to his horror that the blacksmith was herding him towards the mouth of the well. "It can't be easy melting it down on your own."

"True." Shadowjack shifted the knife from one hand to the other, still moving towards the boy. "I have to fetch wood and coal for the fire but I don't like to leave the vault for more than a few minutes, in case someone stumbles on my little operation. That makes the job slow going."

"How many horseshoes have you made in the last month?"

"Six."

"I take your point." Peazle was at the edge of the well mouth now. He could hear the gurgle of the water below and feel cold air rising at his back.

"What if you had help?" he asked quickly. "You could be finished before you knew it."

"Help?" Shadowjack stopped and raised a thick black eyebrow.

"Suppose I was to go down the well and bring out the silver for you to smelt down. My friend Duncan could be a lookout. He's from the highlands. Nobody can sneak up on him unawares and he's handy with a blade if they did."

Peazle struggled to keep the fear out of his voice and sound as reasonable and business-like as possible.

"Shadowjack, there's enough silver down there to make all three of us wealthy a dozen times over."

The blacksmith tapped the blade against his cheek while Peazle teetered on the edge of the well.

"I agree, lad," he said. "You have a deal."

He shot out a meaty paw and grasped Peazle's hand. The force of his handshake lifted the boy away from the menacing hole and he bounced around on the end of the blacksmith's arm like a rag doll.

"Shadowjack," he said through rattling teeth. "Why didn't those Gypsies come looking for the treasure themselves?"

The shaking stopped.

"No idea, son," the giant blacksmith replied evenly. "Leith's a rough area. Maybe something… unfortunate happened to them."

He let go of the pickpocket's hand and gave a toothy smile.

"Off ye go. Find your pal and come right back. Don't ask any more daft questions."

And Peazle went, still shaking like a leaf.

The Gorrodin-Rath

Charlie shut Peazle's diary with a snap.

"Well, that's that, isn't it?" he snorted. "They took the treasure and buggered off out of Edinburgh. I might have known we wouldn't be lucky enough to find it still down there."

"Don't be so sure." Lilly tapped the dirty old book. "If those guys rode into the sunset with the silver, then why was Peazle's diary in the Underground City?"

Charlie arched an eyebrow. "If I had that much money, a stupid diary would be the last thing on my mind,"

"Even if it implicated you in stealing a fortune?"

"Ah. I never thought of that." Charlie pointed an appreciative finger at Lilly and opened Peazle's diary again. "There's still a bit more…"

Duncan, Shadowjack and myself began removing the silver. I wood take a piece of armour or a sword, carry it to the botom of the well and put it in the bucket. Shadowjack would haul it up, melt it down and beet it into a horseshoe shape. Duncan kept a lookout and fetched food and water and, by this method, working day and nite, we quickly transformed all the silver, until there were only a few pieces left...

Duncan sat on a pile of rags in the doorway of the vault where he and Peazle lived. The chamber was one of the last in this particular tunnel, an ideal place to keep watch, to see if anyone walked past, heading for the hidden staircase. The highlander didn't know why he was bothering. In the week they'd been working, not one person had shown the slightest interest in going anywhere near the blacksmith's vault. A combination of superstition, and an understandable fear of an antisocial brute like Shadowjack, effectively dampened the curiosity of any Underground City dwellers. Even the likes of Merry Andrew stayed away.

Today was the last day of their enterprise. The armour and weapons were almost gone and a huge pile of dirt-covered horseshoes were now piled in the corner of Shadowjack's chamber. The blacksmith had used all his savings to purchase a horse and cart, which was tethered in stables at the Pleasance Meadow, a few hundred yards away. At dusk, the trio would transport the booty to the surface, load it onto the cart and drive it through the city gates, claiming it was a delivery for the cavalry at Ruthven Barracks. Once they were out of Edinburgh, they would turn and head for Glasgow, where crooked merchants would pay a fortune for such an amount of pure silver. And it certainly was pure. In fact, it was the most beautiful material Duncan had ever seen.

Tomorrow he would be a rich man. In a few days, he and Peazle would take their share and he would have the money to buy a plot of land in the highlands.

Yet, he wasn't happy. Everything had to be done in secret, for how could three peasants like himself, Peazle and Shadowjack claim to have honestly come by such a fortune? He would have to leave Edinburgh without telling anyone and adopt another identity, which meant he would never see Heather again. He could not bear to spend his life slaving in some Edinburgh factory, yet what was the use of having land when you could not use your own name? When you had no family or loved ones to share your riches with?

And why shouldn't he take someone? In fact, why couldn't he take Heather? He had always felt he had nothing to offer such a beautiful and talented girl. But soon, he would have enough money for both of them to live comfortably. Surely she must be tired of singing for a living in these cramped and filthy streets? She claimed to be a Gypsy, after all, so must share his love of open skies and uncluttered spaces. He could take her away and look after her properly.

His mind made up, he hurried out of the Underground City to find Heather, leaving Shadowjack and Peazle working, unawares, in the darkness below.

Shadowjack put on thick leather gloves and grasped the sides of the giant smelting dish, bubbling above the forge, hooked on a metal pole suspended between two wooden tripods. The blacksmith carefully tipped the container until a small amount of molten silver trickled into a curved iron mould on the vault floor. When it began to harden, he plucked the silver from the mould with iron tongs and hammered it into a proper horseshoe. Sparks drifted through the air and singed the smith's beard, but he was used to this and paid no heed. Like Duncan, he was deep in thought.

It was a shame to have to split all these lovely spoils with the boys. Then again, he had to admit Peazle and Duncan worked hard. He certainly couldn't have pulled the job off without them. Besides, that Duncan was a tough character and Peazle wasn't stupid.

Ach, it was only money, after all. He just needed enough to get to America, find some unclaimed land and open his own smithy, for that was the work he loved. Shadowjack held up the finished horseshoe, swept it through a pile of soot and dirt and plunged it into the bucket of water, causing a mighty blast of steam to rise into the air.

Peazle sat at the bottom of the rock pile, trying to draw a proper lungful of air. In the last few days, his breathing had become more laboured and bouts of coughing racked his frail body. The boy's health was rapidly declining and he suspected he had tuberculosis.

Yet he had to keep going. Until he had a share of the treasure, he couldn't afford medical treatment. Thank goodness there were only a couple of pieces left.

He struggled to his feet but another fit of coughing forced the boy back to his knees. He wiped the back of one hand across his trembling mouth and it came away smeared red. The pickpocket clenched his fists, gritted his bloody teeth, and made himself stand. He picked up a helmet and, with a breathless sob, staggered back into the tunnel.

Heather was singing at the bottom of Blair Street, as she always seemed to be. It occurred to Duncan that, for a Gypsy, she seemed remarkably fond of staying in one spot. She saw him as he came down the hill, quickly finished her song and waved goodbye to the clapping gents. She gave Duncan a hug, standing on tiptoe to get her arms round his neck.

"Hey stranger," she said breathlessly. "I haven't seen you all week."

"Work, work, work, that's me." The highlander replied solemnly. He motioned for the girl to sit beside him. "Heather, I think we need tae talk."

"I thought you were ignoring me." She smiled and hunkered down. "Why so serious? Oh, I forgot. You're always serious."

The highlander smiled at the mild rebuke and took her hand.

"What would you dae if you had enough money to get out of Edinburgh?"

"I don't. Have enough money, that is."

"Suppose I got it."

"I've lived too long in this city to make wishes."

"I might... be on tae something." Duncan ran a hand through his long dark hair, unsure of how to finish. "Something that will make me… well… awfy rich."

"What are you talking about? Have you broken the law? Are you in trouble?"

"Oh, for goodness sakes!" The highlander thumped a hand on his knee. "I've aye been a plain speaker for I dinnae ken any other way."

He clasped her by the shoulders.

"Me and Peazle found treasure. At the bottom of the Underground City, under an auld well. We've almost finished taking it out and it's enough to make us all..."

His voice trailed away. Heather's face had gone white.

"What's wrong?"

"Treasure?" She put a trembling hand on the highlander's knee. "At the bottom of a well?"

"Incredible, isn't it?"

"Is it silver? Weapons and armour made of silver?"

"Aye, that's right." The highlander's delight turned to puzzlement. "Wait a minute. How did you ken that?"

"Duncan. We *do* need to talk."

Shadowjack saw the rope suspended over the well jerk several times, a sign that Peazle was pulling at the other end. He put down his tongs and walked over to the hole.

"How many more, lad?" he shouted down.

"I've tied on a helmet. You can pull it up now." Peazle sounded exhausted. "There's only a shield left, but it's bigger than all the other pieces." There was a fit of coughing from the darkness. "I don't know that I can carry it, Shadowjack. It looks awful heavy."

"Go back to rockfall and have a rest, wee man," Shadowjack shouted back. "I'll melt this piece, then climb down the rope and help you."

"Will do."

The helmet clanked back and forth against the sides of the shaft as the blacksmith pulled it up. When it reached the top, he leaned over the well mouth and untied it. As he finished unfastening the knot, a blast of frigid air hit him, rising from the black depths. Shadowjack shivered violently and dropped the helmet, then peered into the hole, bemused. He had been working in this vault, hauling water and bits of armour out of the shaft, for three long months and had never felt slightly cold before. Now, for some reason, the hairs were standing up on the back of his neck and his calloused skin was covered in goosebumps.

Peazle trudged back to the rockpile and lowered himself onto the floor. It seemed far chillier down here than it had ever been before. He set his aching back against a boulder, stretching and twisting to try and relieve the pain in his tired muscles. He picked up a little flask of whisky Shadowjack had given him and took a sip.

"Whooooeeeegh. Eugh! Eugh! Eeeeeeeeeugh!" He shuddered, putting it quickly down again. "I can't believe people drink this stuff for fun."

But he had to admit Shadowjack's 'medicine' had warmed him a little.

There was a sharp noise to his left and his head jerked up. A small stone tumbled down the rock pile and landed a few feet away. Peazle sighed in relief, unclenching his fists.

"I will be so happy when I get out of this place," he wheezed, sinking back. "My imagination is starting to get the better of me."

"We Gypsies know many stories, Duncan." Heather looked the highlander straight in the eye. "And, to be honest, most are just make-believe. Others we do not take lightly."

"It's the same in the highlands," Duncan agreed. "What of it?"

"There is a legend," she continued in whispered tones, "That I think you should hear about. According to the Gypsies, many centuries ago, one of the Little People was a great magician called Gorrodin.

"Little People again, is it?" Duncan frowned.

"Gorrodin was exiled from Galhadria for a reason I do not know. But his heart was filled with bitterness and he decided that, if he could not live in his own land, he would set up a kingdom on earth."

Lilly pointed to Arthur's Seat, always ominously present over Edinburgh's rooftops.

"In a great cavern under that hill, he created an army called the Gorrodin-Rath and favoured them with a cup, called the Grail, that bestowed eternal life on anyone who drank from it. But it also turned them into monsters. They terrorised the humans who lived in the area and, though the Little People disapproved of what Gorrodin was doing, they did nothing. Magical creatures do not fight each other, you see."

"Why not?" Duncan asked sourly. "We humans dinnae have a problem killing our own."

"I only know that this is a rule Galhadrians dare not break. They must not go to war with each other." She shrugged cynically. "Even if that rule did not exist, Little People love only music, dancing and merriment. They do not much care about men."

Duncan could see the reasoning behind that.

"Gorrodin had a daughter," Heather continued. "Who could not bear to see the evil done by one of her own kin. When a Scots army gathered to fight the Gorrodin-Rath, she led them to a hidden cache of faerie silver, knowing full well that it was deadly to the dark creatures. The Scots forged it into weapons and armour, including a magnificent sword called Excalibur. This was given to the Scots leader Arturius."

"Excalibur? Arturius?" Duncan interrupted. "You mean King Arthur? I thought he was just a myth."

"It's myths we speak of," Heather said. "You must decide whether this one is true."

"Then carry on." Duncan nodded solemnly.

"Some of the Scots led a night raid on the Gorrodin-Rath's stronghold and stole the magic cup. When the creatures - led by their mighty war chief, Mordred, gave chase - they were met by Arturius and the rest of his warriors. Mordred's army couldn't harm those Scots who wore silver armour and could themselves be killed by warriors wielding weapons made from faerie silver. Even so, the Scots were vastly outnumbered and the battle raged through the night until only a few fighters were alive on either side. The Gorrodin-Rath were denizens of the dark so, when dawn broke, they fled through a tunnel into a cavern under Arthur's Seat."

She looked towards the top of the grassy peak.

"Arturius, though mortally wounded, led his few remaining men into the mountain after them. They sealed the entrance to the cavern with rocks and placed their silver weapons and armour in front, as a barrier to stop the Gorrodin-Rath ever getting out. Even Excalibur was left there. It was a barrier the Gorrodin-Rath could not cross, for they dare not touch it."

Duncan paled.

"The Scots searched and found another exit, so they melted down a few pieces of faerie silver and set them in a stout door to seal that too. As a final precaution, they erected a fort at the entrance to always be ready, if the Gorrodin-Rath got out. That fort eventually became Edinburgh Castle."

Lilly indicated the slope in the distance.

"Knowing he was defeated, Gorrodin vanished to the remote north and left his minions to their terrible fate."

"What happened to the Grail?" the highlander asked. "What became of the daughter?"

"Nobody remembers," Heather said simply. "Over hundreds of years, the treasure, the tunnel and Arthur drifted into legend - and the city of Edinburgh was built on top of them."

Heather bit her lip.

"If the tale is true, then it's not treasure that you're removing. It's the bars of an ancient prison."

She held out a hand.

"Duncan, I'm sorry…"

But the highlander was already on his feet and running towards the Underground City.

The Battle

Peazle stood up and stamped his feet. It was definitely much colder, too chilly to sit around any longer. At least, that's what he tried to tell himself. In fact, he felt incredibly vulnerable, sitting in a flickering pool of firebrand light. He hoped Shadowjack was almost finished smelting the helmet. The pickpocket breathed in and, this time, he didn't cough. If he was careful and took things gently, he could probably get that last shield back to the bottom of the well on his own. A few steps then a rest, then a few steps. The hardest part would be getting it from the top of the rockpile. He'd just wait a couple more minutes to get his strength back, then he would give it a go…

Duncan raced through the Underground City, moving over the dark and uneven floor with the grace of a natural hunter. He powered into Shadowjack's vault and cleared the fiery forge with one leap, his foot catching the astonished blacksmith in the centre of his chest. The blow, with the force of a fifty-yard run behind it, caught the giant by surprise - and he toppled backwards with a grunt. As he crashed to the floor, Shadowjack lifted the heavy tongs to strike the boy, but Duncan's knife glinted in the firelight, right below the smith's left eye.

"You make one move," the highlander spat, his face inches from the blacksmith's own. "And you'll never see the money you so badly wish tae spend."

"What is this treachery?" Shadowjack let go of the tongs and held up his empty hand. "Tell me quick. I've always played fair with you."

"You didnae warn us about the monsters!" Duncan wrapped his fingers in the blacksmith's bristling beard and pulled him even closer. "That's why the Gypsies you overheard never came looking for the treasure, isn't it? You told us about the silver, you treacherous dog, but you didnae tell us about the monsters!"

"Monsters!" the giant roared. "What are you babbling about, boy?"

"The silver guards a great evil! It cannae be taken oot!"

"Pah!" The blacksmith's eyes were almost bulging out of his head. "That stupid fairy tale? Only an ignorant peasant would believe something like that. I didn't even think it worth mentioning!"

"I believe in fairy stories," Duncan hissed. He lifted himself off Shadowjack's chest and stood up, still brandishing the knife. "I lost my brother tae the Little People. I'm not going tae lose my best friend too."

"You're brave to anger a man like me, highlander." Shadowjack sat up, his face red with rage. "Also very foolish."

He struggled to his feet and stepped forward, towering over Duncan.

"If I'm wrong, then I apologise to you, blacksmith, and my shame will be great." Duncan tucked his knife back into a leather sheath under his arm. "But I fear the worst."

"Nonsense!" Shadowjack fumed. "I'm on my way down to help Peazle take out the last piece of treasure right now. When we've brought it up, I want to hear no more of this ignorant tomfoolery."

"The last piece? Already?"

"Aye," Shadowjack scowled. "We're not all sitting around, thinking up daft children's tales, you know. That boy down there is working like a dog."

"Shadowjack, I beg you to trust me on this." Duncan moved to the well. "Stoke up the fire as high as it will go. Please."

He sat on the edge and grasped the rope.

"I'll explain when I return. If I'm being foolish, you can laugh at me while you count your money."

A self-mocking smile played on his lips, but his eyes burned into Shadowjack's with an intensity that made the blacksmith suddenly look down. Duncan slid over the well rim and into the darkness.

Shadowjack stood for a few minutes staring at the black hole and stroking his beard. Then he turned and began to quickly pile wood on the forge.

The shield made a grinding noise as Peazle slid it down the rock pile, but he knew the silver would be undamaged by the jagged stone. He had once overheard a learned gent claim that precious metals scratched and broke easily but this stuff seemed indestructible. Peazle was beginning to doubt these learned gents were ever right about anything. The shield slid off the last rock and hit the floor with a clang. The pickpocket began to drag it down the passage that led to the bottom of the well.

He had gone about fifty yards when it occurred to him that he had left Shadowjack's liquor flask back at the rockpile. Sighing, he trudged back to get it. He was stuffing the container inside his shirt when he heard footsteps pounding up the corridor in his direction.

"No need to hurry Shadowjack, I'm managing just fine." He looked round as a running figure emerged from the darkness. "Duncan! What are you doing down here?"

The highlander slowed to a halt, his chest heaving.

"You all right?"

"Why wouldn't I be? Apart from coughing a bit, I'm fit as…."

Peazle's reply was drowned out by a deafening crack. A huge slab of stone shot out of the rock pile, like a cork from a champagne bottle, shattering into a thousand pieces on the cavern wall opposite. Duncan launched himself at Peazle, knocking the boy over and flattening him to the ground. The firebrand spun into the air and clattered across the floor as pieces of boulder rained down around them. A chunk the size of a brick hit Duncan between the shoulders and a thousand points of pain burst across the back of his head. He slumped forward on top of the pickpocket.

"Duncan! You're squashing me!" Peazle tried to roll the half-conscious highlander off, then froze as he peered from under his friend's motionless body.

An arm jutted out of a hole where the rock had been. It was long, powerful and twice the size of one of Shadowjack's powerful limbs. But this arm was so white it was almost translucent - hairless, with thick blue veins and spattered with patches of grey mould. And the hand on the end! It was more like a claw, curved, twitching and bristling with vicious yellow talons.

"Heaven save us!" Peazle whispered, thumping his groggy friend on the shoulder. "Duncan! Get up! Pleeeeeeeeeeeeeeease!"

With a shudder, the rocks around the arm rose and parted and a head and shoulders burst out.

Peazle screamed.

The cranium was bald and misshapen, eyes sunk so far into the creature's doughy flesh, they were no more than malevolent little beads. The monster pulled its body slowly out of the gap, squat, wide and bent almost double - as if an eternity of squeezing through low passages had permanently curved the massive, knotted spine. It opened a cavernous mouth, revealing two rows of jagged teeth and stepped down from the rock pile, almost daintily. Its powerful sinewy legs ended in hooves, rather than feet.

Another head, equally ugly, burst from the rocks a few feet away.

"We have to get out of here!" Peazle hissed, twisting his friend's head in the direction of the aberrations and slapping his face. "Wake up!"

Duncan finally got his eyes to focus. With a grunt of agony, he pushed himself groggily to his feet, pulling Peazle with him. By now, a third, smaller creature had forced its way through the stones and the first two were clear of the rock pile, standing on the chamber floor itself.

"What in God's name are they?" Peazle whimpered.

"Gorrodin-Rath." Imminent danger had sharpened Duncan's senses, despite the pain. "We cannae let them get between us and the way back."

The monsters were crouching and stretching, sniffing the air and each other. Grabbing Peazle's hand, the highlander began to inch along the wall. "They dinnae seem to see very well, which is a wee blessing."

The two closest trolls glanced at the children and then over at the exit. With ugly leering grins, they moved to block off the boy's retreat.

"Nothing wrong with their hearing, pal." Peazle tried to shrink back further into the shadows, but it was too late. The third troll joined his companions and a fourth was beginning to emerge from the rocks.

"It's nae use. We're trapped." Duncan pulled out his knife and held it valiantly in front of them. "When I attack, you run to the right. Follow the wall. You'll only have a few seconds."

"When you attack!" Peazle grabbed his friend's arm. "Are you insane?"

"Nae point in both of us dying," Duncan said calmly, despite his racing heart. "Go tae the right, as I say."

The beasts looked at each other and one snorted loudly. The boys could smell a blast of foetid breath, for the nearest couldn't be more than twelve feet away.

"What if they understand Scots?" Peazle stammered. "You've just told them which way I'm going to go."

"Then choose your own path! Surprise me!"

"No, Duncan." The pickpocket picked up a chunk of broken stone. "You're my only friend and, by my soul, we'll live or die together."

The trolls edged towards the boys, hooves clicking on the stone floor and thin black lips curling back over drooling fangs. They hunched down and stretched their claws out - grunting, panting and waving their heads from side to side, in a sinister, snake-like motion. Duncan shifted the knife from hand-to-hand.

"Goodbye, Peazle," he said gently.

With a mighty roar, Shadowjack Henry barrelled into the cavern, swinging the silver shield around his head. The corner caught the troll nearest to him and half its malformed head vanished in a black oily cloud. The other creatures spun round, releasing a cacophony of ear splitting screams, recoiling when they caught sight of the gleaming silver.

"To me, lads!" Shadowjack raced across the vault. The shield connected with the outstretched claw of one of the trolls and sliced it clean off - a white clutching hand flew through the air and landed at Peazle's feet. Galvanised, he and Duncan darted over to where Shadowjack was swinging the shield back and forth. At each thrust the monsters shrank away, waving their arms ineffectually.

"Duncan, my boy," the blacksmith roared as the boys sheltered behind him. "I've decided there's no need for you to apologise, after all."

"Glad tae hear it," Duncan said as the trio began backing into the tunnel. "Now give me that shield."

"What?"

"Shadowjack, you said you'd trust me! Give it to me, then I need you to do exactly what I say."

Duncan grabbed the shield before the blacksmith could object.

"Run back to the well. Take Peazle, though you might have tae carry him."

Peazle was stumbling alongside them, coughing violently again.

"I've nae time to explain, but I have a plan. Climb back up to the vault and start melting the silver horseshoes in thon forge."

"Why? I mean… how many?"

"All of them, Shadowjack, or else we're dead. Go!"

The blacksmith looked like he was about to object, when another unearthly scream of rage rose from the chamber they had just left. Instead, he scooped Peazle under one meaty arm and set off. Duncan turned and faced the direction of the enemy, shield in hand, as the pursuing trolls clattered into the tunnel. Stopping when they saw his defence, they hissed, spat and screamed, yet dared not go any further. Duncan was facing his worst nightmare and felt like collapsing with pain and terror. But he was a boy with a long line of warriors' blood in his veins.

"Right, ye big Sassenach devils!" he yelled, for want of anything more appropriate to say. "Let's see you take on a highlander! Aye, you, wi your pasty faces and bad breath!"

The trolls retreated a few feet, snarling and gurgling amongst themselves. Bent and bloated bodies almost filled the corridor and Duncan could see at least five of them crowding behind the leader. Two of the monsters turned and loped away, the tapping of their hooves fading into the distance. The highlander knew immediately what they were up to, for there were many branching corridors in this labyrinth. His adversaries were going to circle round and find another route to the well, catching Peazle and Shadowjack unawares and cutting off his own retreat.

There was nothing else for it. With a blood-curdling yell, Duncan charged at the enemy, catching the three remaining trolls off guard. Fleeing in panic, they tried to scramble over each other, spitting and clawing, in an attempt to get away. Their bodies were too large to manoeuvre properly in such a confined space and Duncan swung the shield, catching the nearest creature square in the back. A huge gout of black liquid arched from between its shoulders as it fell, writhing and screaming. His second swing took the upraised arm from the second before the monsters thundered, squealing in terror, back the way they had come.

Duncan shouldered the shield, spun on his heel, and headed in the direction Shadowjack had gone.

Peazle was standing, knee-deep in water, at the bottom of the well, when Duncan reached the chamber.

"Shadowjack's climbed the rope to the top and is melting the horseshoes back down again," he sputtered weakly. "Seems a shame, after all the effort we put into making them."

"Then get up there after him! These beasties will be here any second and I cannae hold them all off, no even with a silver shield."

The pickpocket shook his head.

"I haven't got the strength to climb, Duncan. Besides, I thought you might need this." He thrust his arm into the black water and pulled out a beautiful silver sword.

"Where in the name of all that's Holy did you get that?" Duncan gasped.

"Hid it behind a rock a couple of weeks ago." Peazle tossed him the weapon. "Out of pure greed, y'know?"

Duncan looked at the sword reverently.

"My friend, ye never cease tae amaze me."

The bucket and rope came tumbling down the funnel and splashed into the water, narrowly missing the pickpocket.

"The horseshoes are melting away just fine," Shadowjack's voice echoed down. "Grab hold of the rope, lad."

"Take the shield with you." Duncan thrust it out. "Melt it down too. Melt everything that's silver. Then throw the rope back for me."

Too weak to protest, Peazle hoisted the shield on his back and sat on the bucket.

"Haul away, Shadowjack!"

Boy, bucket and shield rose, unhesitatingly, into the air - Duncan could hear Shadowjack grunting as he pulled. The highlander spun, sword in hand, in time to see the first beast slither into the chamber. Then another entered. And another. And another, until twelve of the monstrosities were bunched together in the vault. One gestured violently and the creatures began to fan out, gurgling and slobbering. They inched in both directions along the chamber wall until, eventually, they ringed the highlander. Duncan circled on the spot, holding out the sword, but knew he had lost. He could kill five or six, perhaps even more. In the end, however, they would overcome him by sheer weight of numbers.

The bucket landed in the water again and the trolls recoiled in surprise. That was the spilt second Duncan needed. He rammed his foot into it and grasped the rope with one hand.

"Pull, Shadowjack! Pull, or my life is over!"

Shadowjack gave a tremendous roar of exertion from above and Duncan shot into the air. Seeing their victim about to escape, the trolls rushed forwards en masse - the largest leaping into the air towards him, talons outstretched. Duncan swung the sword in a vicious arc and the creature's clawing fingers were sliced from its hand. The monster fell back into the water with a cry.

"You beasties are no gonnae hae any limbs left by the time we finish with you!" the boy shouted triumphantly, as he vanished up the funnel.

Peazle was waiting at the top to help Duncan clamber out of the well and into Shadowjack's vault. He gasped at the clouds of steam enveloping them - for the blacksmith had simply dumped the huge smelting dish onto the red-hot coals of his forge, then thrown in all the silver. The highlander could see the shield dissolving into a mass of bubbling molten metal that almost reached the top of the huge container. Shadowjack gave a whistle when he saw the sword.

"That's a piece and a half, no mistake. Can't believe we missed it the first time." He eyed the weapon hungrily. "You sure you want it melted down as well?"

"I dinnae think we'd better." Duncan held up the weapon in awe. "I'm wondering if this might be the legendary Excalibur itself."

"Aye. Right."

"I'll wager on it!"

"You have nothing left to wager with!"

"Could we get back to your plan, Duncan, whatever it is?" Peazle peered into the well. "These things are climbing."

"Tip out the molten silver." The highlander pointed to the dish. "Tip it doon the shaft."

"No!" Shadowjack held up his hands in horror. "That's our fortune!"

"And how will you spend it from your grave?"

Shadowjack groaned in disbelief, then grabbed a stout cudgel leaning against the wall. He rammed it into the glowing coals below the dish.

"Help me, then. Quick now, before this goes up in flames!" He leant his considerable weight on the staff and pushed. The boys ran to his side and hauled down on the cudgel as hard as they could. The container creaked slowly and lifted a few inches above the forge.

"Once more, boys. With all your might!"

Duncan and Peazle wrenched down on the staff again, with the desperation of people whose lives hung on a thread. The huge dish rose slowly out of the forge and toppled onto its side. Half a ton of molten silver surged out of the container and flowed into the well.

There was an unholy scream from inside the funnel as liquid metal engulfed the climbing trolls and swept them back into the depths. The creatures that filled the chamber below tried to escape when the molten mass hit the river at the bottom, but it was too late. A giant cloud of vapour, saturated with droplets of silver, filled the vault and shot along the tunnels at the bottom, enveloping the fleeing enemy.

In a matter of seconds, the rest of the Gorrodin-Rath, who had survived for over a millennium, were blasted out of existence.

Shadowjack, Peazle and Duncan lay on their backs in the vault, gasping and laughing with joy.

"We did it!" Shadowjack thumped Duncan on the chest. "Poor as church mice again, aye, but alive all the same."

"No exactly." Duncan held Excalibur above his head. "This thing has a jewel set in it the size of a hen's egg."

"Poor or not poor, let's get out of here." Shadowjack sat up. "I, for one, don't intend to spend another day locked away from daylight. Not so long as I live."

He stretched out his arm, helped Peazle to his feet then reached back for Duncan. As he did so, a mournful howl rose from the depths of the well. It was a sound more powerful, nerve-jangling and, strangely enough, more human than any of the other creatures had made. Shadowjack froze in mid-pull.

"Oh my God." Peazle clutched the blacksmith's arm. "What was that?"

"Their war chief, Mordred, would be my guess," Duncan said flatly. "Clever beastie. He must have stayed well back while the rest attacked."

"How do you know all this stuff?"

"Never mind that. What will we do?"

"Whatever it is, we better make it quick!"

Shadowjack hauled Duncan to his feet with a mighty tug. The trio could hear hoofbeats growing louder, rattling down the tunnel towards the bottom of the well.

Mordred was coming.

"The dish!" The pickpocket indicated the container lying on its side. "It's still lined with silver. Looks like it might just fit in the well."

"Only one way to find out." Shadowjack flexed his mighty arms, picked up the container with a muscle-popping heave and slammed it into the hole in the vault floor. It slid down almost to its brim, where the lip prevented it sinking any further. Shadowjack stepped back, waving his hands in the air.

"Ooooh." He said through gritted teeth. "Still a bit hot, that."

"There's enough silver left crusted on the bottom of the dish to stop what's down there ever getting out."

Mordred knew it too. There was another venomous roar from below, then the rat-tat-tat of Mordred's hooves thundering back down the passage, as the monster searched in vain for another exit from the lower level. Duncan pushed at the smelting container with his foot but it didn't budge.

"You think there's any way that... thing can get out?"

"I doubt it." Peazle shuddered. "I imagine the soldiers intended to fill in the tunnel at the other end and, anyway, it's sealed halfway with a silver-studded door."

"What if someone removes the dish?"

"This vault already has a bad enough reputation. After all that unearthly screaming and drumming, I can't see anyone ever coming near it again."

"Just in case, we can block up the stairs that lead down here," Shadowjack said.

"Wait a minute." Peazle went to the back of the vault and fetched his journal. "Whatever that thing trapped down there might be, it's lived for a long, long time and isn't likely to die any day soon."

He opened the book and began to write.

"Gather as many loose rocks as you can to hide the well. I'm going to leave my diary here as a warning, in case anyone ever finds this place again."

Shadowjack and Duncan silently scoured the vault and adjoining corridors for suitable debris while Peazle completed his journal. They wrapped the book in one of a Shadowjack's smelting gloves, left it in the dish, pulled a plank over the top and covered it with stones.

"I said you'd write something important one day." Duncan patted Peazle on the shoulder. The pickpocket didn't smile.

"I pity the poor soul who finds it," he said dolefully.

Then, with Excalibur wrapped in an old oilskin cloth, Peazle, Duncan and Shadowjack Henry walked out of the Underground City and into the sunlight.

The Bodysnatcher

Charlie turned the page but there was nothing else written in the book. He flicked through the rest of Peazle's diary but, from that point on, the pages were blank. He stood up, ignoring Lilly, and paced around the theatre floor. The girl sat and waited, running a small silver ball over her fingers, from one hand to another. Finally, Charlie turned to her, tight-lipped.

"There's no way I'm believing that," he burst out. "There's no way I'm accepting there's some kind of monster still trapped at the bottom of the Underground City."

Lilly stayed quiet.

"I know what you're thinking," the boy continued. "That tapping I heard underground was the sound of Mordred's hooves. You think he heard me and came running up the passage below."

"You don't know what I think."

"Well, it's rubbish. That noise was council workers digging, just like you said."

"Could be." Lilly shrugged. "I wasn't down there."

"I don't believe in that kind of stuff! The journal must be a hoax."

"Sit down, Charlie," Lilly sighed. "Trying to make sense of this and walk at the same time is freaking you out."

The boy slouched back down and patted his knees, nervously blowing out his cheeks.

"Look," he said, after a while. "Just suppose the diary is right. I'm just saying suppose, I'm not saying it is."

He began to get up again but Lilly pulled him back.

"Then let's suppose," she said. "What are you going to do?"

"Make sure nobody ever finds Shadowjack's vault again. Mordred's still trapped, isn't he? I'll go down and cover the smelting forge and… eh… I'll hide the stairway I found that leads to the vault. Put the stones back. Put everything back the way it was."

He smiled hopefully at the girl.

"If there is some sort of horrible creature down there, that'll keep him hidden for another two hundred years."

"I suppose it would," said Lilly. "If it wasn't for the fact that there are going to be council workers digging towards him. If they break through to the bottom level, Mordred will surely kill them."

"That guy stays angry a long time, eh?"

"Worse still. He'll be out."

"Couldn't we tell the police or the army or something?" the boy suggested.

"Tell them what? That you discovered a thousand-year-old troll living under the streets of Edinburgh? They're not likely to believe that."

"I know the feeling."

"You have to do something."

"So what if he does get out?" Charlie was clutching at straws now. "How dangerous can he be? Magic or not, he's only one creature. This is the 21st century. The army has rockets and bombs and stuff."

"We're in the middle of a heavily populated city." The girl looked deep into his eyes. "What if he breaks out when your parents are performing in the big top?"

"What do you expect me to do?" Charlie leapt to his feet. "Take him on at hand-to-hand combat? I'm only a kid."

Lilly pointed to Peazle's diary.

"Two boys about your age once managed to beat a whole army of trolls."

"They had the help of a magic sword and a blacksmith the size of Mount Everest!"

With a flick of her wrist, Lilly sent the silver ball whizzing towards Charlie's head. He plucked the object out of the air, an inch from his nose, blinking in surprise.

"What the hell did you do that for?"

"Your parents are acrobats, you said? Look at how easily you caught the ball. You've inherited their speed and their eye."

"I'd rather my parents were big-game hunters and I'd inherited their guns. Am I supposed to fight this thing with my teeth?" He gave the girl a sarcastic sneer. "I've got silver fillings. Think that'll help?"

Lilly didn't get the joke.

"Only faerie silver will work against these kind of creatures, though you're on the right track. You have to think of what you have on your side, not what you don't."

"I've got you. Want to come into the Underground City with me?"

"Not a chance."

"Thought not," the boy said dryly, flicking the ball back. "But thanks for your support."

"Charlie, I didn't mean it like that!"

"I got to think about this." The boy strode towards the theatre exit. "I have to go somewhere and work it out."

He opened the door, letting in a flood of sunlight.

"It's not that I'm stupid or a coward. It's just that I'm scared to death and I don't have a clue."

He stepped into the light without bothering to say goodbye. The door closed with a click, leaving Lilly sitting alone in the gloomy big top. She took out some more silver balls and began to juggle them - thirteen, then fifteen, then seventeen, spinning faster and faster, despite the half-light. One of the silver balls hit the edge of her finger and shot away at an awkward angle. She tried to recapture her momentum clutching at empty air, but another ball deflected off her wrist and vanished under a chair. Next moment, all the orbs were bouncing across the floor, away from the distraught girl.

Lilly looked at her hands sadly.

"I can't help him," she whispered to nobody in particular. "That's not fair at all."

Charlie was sitting in his room at the boarding house, staring at the wall and trying to formulate a plan, when his parents trooped in

"It's Wednesday tomorrow," his father announced. "Big Top's shut, so we thought about taking you on a day trip. There's a pencil museum in Lerwick."

"I'd love to go," Charlie said.

"Really? You would?"

"Yes, but I can't." The boy thought fast. "I… eh… have to meet a girl."

"Young love, eh?" His father grinned. "You think a girl will be more fun than the pencil museum?"

"Don't tease him," Charlie's mum somersaulted onto the bed beside her son and they both bounced up and down for a few seconds. "What would you like to know about the facts of life?"

"Nothing, mother. We'll probably just go for a coke."

"That's nice." His mother nudged him, wrinkling her nose. "Do you think about her a lot?"

"As a matter of fact, I've thought about nothing else for hours." Charlie looked up at the woman. "And I'm pretty sure she hasn't been very honest."

"Aw, baby." His mum suddenly looked serious, which didn't happen very often. "Are you going to be all right? You want to talk about it?"

For a second, Charlie considered telling his parents the whole story. He could give them Peazle's journal to read, then climb into bed and go to sleep. Let them work out what was real, what was not - and what he should do about it.

He looked at his father hopefully. His dad made a high whinnying noise, his cheeks vibrating violently.

"That's my impression of a horse," he said. "I can only do it from one side of my mouth."

Charlie groaned.

"It's fine," he said, patting his mother's hand. "Everything's OK."

"Have a talk with this young lady, son. Never let anyone walk all over you."

"I don't intend to."

"Good. Well, you have a fun time tomorrow. Dad and I can have a long lie and go shopping instead."

Charlie's dad sighed.

Finally, his parents went to bed and left Charlie to his thoughts. He desperately wanted to believe Peazle's diary was fake and that magic didn't exist. But he had seen these events, not just read them. What's more, he was convinced Lilly knew more than she was telling.

She should have been as surprised and horrified as he was. Instead, she calmly accepted it all.

Her reactions just didn't ring true.

He felt betrayed and even more lonely. He had come to think of Peazle and Duncan as friends and, now the diary was finished, he would never know what happened to them. Did they take Excalibur to Glasgow and sell it? Did they become rich like they dreamed? Or had Peazle succumbed to the illness that was obviously killing him?

He took out the note and read it again.

If you are reading this you are in mortal danger. Take the book, leev now and cover your tracks. I pray you are brave at hart and of good character and, if so, read on then do what you must. Hopefuly, at the end, you will find a way to emerge victorious.

"Not very helpful," Charlie scoffed. "I don't see a way to emerge victorious in the end. Couldn't you just have given me some bloody instructions?"

He frowned.

For Peazle hadn't written 'in the end'. The note said, 'at the end'. And though the pickpocket was a terrible speller, there was nothing wrong with his grammar.

Charlie's jaw dropped.

"It can't be that simple."

He opened the pickpocket's diary and flicked through it again. At the end was his hand-drawn map of Greyfriars graveyard. There were little ticks scattered across the page, presumably marking the sites of recently buried corpses, ripe for stealing. Looking closer, he saw that one plot was marked with a tiny cross rather than a tick.

He held the book closer and peered at the minuscule marking. Was it a cross?

Or was it a sword?

Charlie leapt to his feet, opened the boarding house window and climbed onto the sill. Without a second's pause, he swung out and clambered down the drainpipe. Soon he was walking through the silent, deserted streets once more. He reached the big top, let himself in and felt his way to the little vault in the South Bridge where the workmen kept their tools. He took one of the construction helmets with a light on top, put it on his head and wrapped a short shovel in a splattered paint sheet. Then he let himself out of the theatre and strode through the Old Town until he stood at the gates of Greyfriars Graveyard.

The cemetery looked very different at night. The church seemed to be carved from squat cold shadows and gravestones were scattered like blackened stumps of teeth. Charlie switched on the torch and made his way quietly around the church until he came to the grave of James Hogg, hidden in thick shadow, at the bottom of the building. Hands shaking, he unwrapped the shovel, looking around to see if his actions might be detected. But the graveyard was deserted and all lights were off in the surrounding tenements.

He opened Peazle's journal at the back and studied the exact position of the cross.

"Here we go," the boy muttered, "The last of the body snatchers."

He took a deep breath and plunged the shovel into the soil, a few feet from the flat tombstone.

Nothing. The spade simply sank into the soft ground. Charlie withdrew the tool and pushed it in again a few inches to the left. Again nothing. He tried the right this time and, once more, the spade met no resistance. On the fourth try, the metal hit something solid.

Charlie began to dig around the spot and, a few moments later, could see an object glinting in his helmet beam. The sky was beginning to lighten, so he scraped hurriedly at the dirt and soon uncovered a beautiful, jewel-encrusted sword handle.

Hardly daring to breathe, he bent down, grasped the handle and pulled. Excalibur slid slowly and easily from the soil next to the grave of Peazle's hero and Charlie held the gleaming weapon in front of him.

"You knew!" he laughed, raising the weapon and saluting his companion from the past. "I don't know how you persuaded Shadowjack to part with this, but you knew. Someday, someone would find your diary. Then they'd need the sword."

He sat down on the flat gravestone, looking at the stunning object, and a great feeling of sadness welled up inside him. Partly he was uncertain and scared. Partly he couldn't understand how he had gotten into an incredible situation like this.

But mostly, he grieved for Peazle. If the boy had convinced Shadowjack and Duncan to bury the sword, then he didn't get rich after all. Without money, he wouldn't have been able to afford medicine. Charlie didn't think the pickpocket had lasted much longer after finishing his diary.

The boy felt a welcome warmth at his back as the sun began to rise over the eastern wall of the graveyard. He raised Excalibur above his head and let the rays of a new day dance along its blade.

"Thank you, my friend," he whispered.

He stood up and made a few practice cuts in the air with the weapon. He had no idea how to wield a sword but Excalibur was light and, somehow, felt right in his hand. He edged his way around Hogg's grave, slashing at imaginary foes, imagining he was Arturius, surrounded by the army of Gorrodin-Rath. He clutched his heart.

"You got me, pesky varmints!" he croaked, staggering back and forward. "But, before I die, I'll chase you down these tunnels to the very gates of hell and seal you in."

Charlie stopped, Excalibur quivering in the air.

"Wait a minute. Why would the Gorrodin-Rath retreat into a tunnel, where they knew they could be trapped?" He lowered the sword. "If they were losing, why didn't they just run away?"

He thought back to Peazle's diary.

As dawn broke, the Gorrodin-Rath finally fled and took shelter in the caverns under Arthur's Seat.

Charlie looked up at the golden orb getting higher over the graveyard wall.

As dawn broke.

A grin of comprehension spread slowly across his face. There was something the Gorrodin-Rath feared as much as faerie silver.

They were afraid of daylight.

The Monster

Charlie stepped into the theatre, construction helmet in one hand and paint cloth in the other. Lilly was sitting in the empty front row of chairs, exactly where the boy had left her the evening before. Her face was pale and drawn and she looked like she had been there all night.

"Where's your father, Lilly?" Charlie asked.

"Eh?" The girl was taken aback by this unexpected question. "I don't know."

"I mean, where's your father on that?" The boy pointed to a huge poster adorning the theatre wall. It advertised acts performing at the big top during the festival and was printed in fancy, circus-style lettering.

BLACK HART ENTERTAINMENT PRESENTS:
THE EDINBURGH FESTIVAL ACROBATIC CIRCUS!

The Flying Pollock Brothers
Bert the Human Bullet
The Bouncing Brucies
Skulina: Mistress of the Wire
The Wonderful Wilsons

Dazzling Derek and Deekie Bob the Wonder Dog

"I remember my dad telling me this attraction is just for acrobats, apart from Deekie Bob the Wonder Dog, of course." He walked over and studied the poster more closely. "I thought your father was supposed to be a magician performing in this big top, but I don't see him advertised."

"It must be a typo," Lilly shrugged.

"How did you know ordinary silver wouldn't work against Mordred?" Charlie kept going.

"What are you talking about?"

"Yesterday, you said only faerie silver could beat Mordred. But you hadn't read that part of the book, so how did you know?" Charlie strode towards her. "How come I never see you anywhere except inside this theatre?"

"Why are you hounding me like this?" Lilly backed away.

"You said your father is a great magician. Where is he?"

"Stop!" The girl held up her hands but the boy kept advancing.

"You're Gorrodin's daughter, aren't you? The girl who led the Scots to the faerie silver." He pointed an accusing finger. "I imagine you're also Heather, the singer Duncan liked so much."

Lilly went white.

"You're one of the Little People." Charlie shook his head and laughed mirthlessly. "Now, *there's* a phrase I never thought I'd hear myself say."

"You seem to have it all worked out." Lilly managed to sound impressed and resentful at the same time.

"Actually, it was a guess." The boy looked sheepish.

"It was a good guess."

"Why didn't you tell me right away?"

"Oh, I don't know." Lilly pulled a face. "Probably cause you'd think I was nuts. You had to read Peazle's book before you'd believe."

"You put a spell on me. That's why I was able to witness what happened in the past whenever I opened the diary."

"You said you didn't like reading."

"Fair enough." To the girl's surprise, Charlie chuckled. It seemed like nothing was impossible anymore. He would just have to get used to it.

"The diary said Heather had dark hair but yours is red. I suppose that's magic too?"

"No, it was dirt. You think 19th century Gypsies could afford shampoo?"

This time Charlie laughed, then reached out and took her arm. She flinched as if she wasn't used to being accepted.

"It's fine. Sit beside me." Despite her deceit, the boy found it impossible to stay angry with Lilly. Besides, he needed answers fast. Any information he could get from the girl might now save his life. He flopped down on a chair and she sat next to him, looking at the floor.

"Why have you stayed here so long?" Charlie asked. "Why don't you live in Galhadria with the rest of the Little People?"

"I can't go back. Not after what my father did."

"Where exactly is he?"

"I really don't know." The girl wouldn't look up. "He deserted me long ago and hasn't been seen since."

"I'm sorry about that." Charlie took her hand.

"I loved him, you know. But I had to try and make right the great wrong he did."

"Are you telling me you've hung around the entrance to the Underground City for millennia?" The boy squinted at her. "Just to stop Mordred and his gang getting out?"

"Partly because of that." The girl put a trembling hand to her mouth. "I also thought, someday, my father might come back."

"I got to admire your patience." Charlie gave her hand a squeeze.

"I like living in Edinburgh," She waved her hand dismissively. "And I want revenge, no matter how long it takes."

"Lilly," the boy said, evenly as he could. "If you're a magician's daughter and one of the Little People, why didn't you use your powers to fight Mordred? Why are you trying to make me do it instead?"

Lilly finally looked up, her eyes wide and green.

"Magical creatures must not fight other magical creatures. It's a law so old, we no longer even think about it." She leaned forward earnestly. "But I know if I break it, something terrible will happen."

She shook her head miserably.

"I can't help you."

"I know, I know." The boy couldn't hide his irritation. "And Little People don't care much for humans either. You like to dance and sing."

He curled his lip.

"For a magical race, you Galhadrians don't actually do an awful lot."

"You're not even supposed to know we exist." Lilly gripped her mortal companion's hand so tightly that the boy winced. "Charlie, I'm doing my best! I've kept people out of Mordred's way for centuries. Now I'm trying to save the lives of these workmen."

"Yeah. By sending some kid to take on Toothy Mctoothface."

"No. There's something different about you. I don't know what it is - but it's sort of… magical as well."

"Aw, you're giving me a big head." Charlie grinned again. "Look, he's just one creature. We call in a bomb threat and the army will be here in no time. They're bound to make short work of him."

"Not unless they have bullets made of faerie silver," Lilly sighed deeply. "And you're missing the point. Mordred is proof that magic exists. If he gets out, your whole race will believe, once again. And men are far more advanced than they used to be. Your scientists might even find a way to make our magic work for *them*."

"Would that be so bad? Could solve a lot of the world's problems."

"You've developed weapons that could destroy your own planet, Charlie. That's *without* spells." Lilly arched an eyebrow. "What do you think?"

She jabbed a thumb at her chest.

"How long would it be before they discovered a way to reach Galhadria and come hunting my people again?"

"I take your point." Charlie picked up the paint cloth and unwrapped Excalibur, its blade glowing a ghostly blue in the dim light of the big top. Lilly gasped when she saw it.

"No point hanging around here then, is there?" He lifted the sword above his head and plunged it back down. The blade sank into the stone floor as if it were made of butter. Charlie let go and Excalibur quivered and sang, vibrating like a huge bee sting.

"I've got a monster to fight."

"Do you have a plan?"

"Sure." Charlie stood up and placed the helmet with the flashlight on his head. "I'm counting on Mordred laughing himself to death when he sees me."

"Let me fix this." Lilly rose and fastened the strap of the hard hat under the boy's chin. She had to stand on her toes to reach and the top half of her body pressed against his chest. She felt cold.

"So, what do I call you?" Charlie said. "A Little Person?"

"You call me a friend," She slid her arms around his waist and gave him a tentative hug, her head resting lightly on his shoulder.

"You have your parent's courage," she whispered in his ear. "Remember, you also have their skill. Use it."

She leaned back and kissed him quickly on the lips, then held him by the shoulders, at arm's length, like a general inspecting one of her troops. Charlie was surprised to see the girl's eyes glistening.

"If I don't manage this…" he began.

Lilly put a finger to his lips.

"These are the first tears I have shed since my father vanished," she said softly. "Please don't die."

Suddenly the boy felt more confident, more powerful and more loved than he ever had in his life. He lifted his hand to touch the girl's cheek, just once, then walked towards the door at the back of the theatre.

"Your sword!" Lilly motioned towards Excalibur, still upright and vibrating.

"I don't need it. Not yet."

Charlie smiled and stepped through the door.

Lilly came back to the weapon and crouched beside it, admiring the intricate carvings on the flawless blade. She clenched her fists in a little gesture of triumph.

"He does have a plan," she said to Excalibur. "I knew he would."

Charlie searched around the little vault where the council workers kept their supplies until he found a small pulley he had noticed on his first visit. He put it in his pocket, took a length of nylon rope from a shelf and wound it around his waist. Then he moved the debris covering the tunnel entrance, slid inside and began crawling back towards the lower levels of the Underground City. He knew he could easily find Shadowjack Henry's vault again. All he had to do was follow the chalk marks he had made on the wall less than a week ago.

He could hardly believe it. Seven days ago, he was an ordinary boy living a normal life. Now he was marching down a hidden tunnel to do battle with an ancient monster. He wasn't the same person anymore, for the old Charlie wouldn't even have stood up to a school bully. But this was not some petty classroom squabble. It was a noble and valiant quest. The kind of thing he had always imagined doing.

He still wasn't sure it was worth fighting a monster for.

When he reached Shadowjack's vault, the boy stood outside the doorway for several minutes until his breathing was under control and his heart had stopped pounding. Once inside the chamber, he would have to work quickly and calmly, if he were to have any chance of succeeding. Or staying alive, for that matter.

"Hesitation is an acrobat's worst enemy," he said to himself and stepped into the chamber.

The hard hat's beam lit up the wooden triangle and iron hook - the old apparatus Shadowjack Henry once used to draw water for his forge. Charlie dragged it to within a few feet of the well, positioning the set-up between the blocked hole and vault doorway. He unwound the rope around his waist, threaded it through the detachable metal pulley he had brought and fastened the pulley to the wooden triangle. He took the end of the rope and tied it to the ancient hook. The metal was rusty but still solid enough for his purpose.

The rope and pulley system now formed the basis for a crude winch and he slid the hook under the rim of the metal cylinder that blocked the well. He stepped back, wound the rest of the rope back around his waist, and began walking towards the exit.

The rope tightened.

Charlie gritted his teeth and kept going. The pulley jiggled and there was a grinding sound from the metal dish. The boy pulled harder, though each tug tightened the rope around his waist and forced air from his lungs. The metal dish groaned again and the rim slid up a few inches. Charlie grunted, trying to find a proper foothold, throwing himself against the rope, fighting for air, sweat prickling his body. His feet slipped with each step, so he seemed to be walking on the spot. He bent his head and strained even more.

The dish rose a foot out of the well.

"Aaaaaaaaaaaaaaaaaaaaargh!" Charlie roared, staggering forwards, fists clenched and veins standing out on his forehead. "Come on! You rotten, stupid… COME ON!"

With a horrendous screech, the container lurched out of the hole in the ground and landed with a crash, demolishing the wooden frame. Charlie collapsed face down, his outstretched hands scraping along the floor, lacerating the skin on his palms. In an instant, he was back on his feet and unwinding the rope. He glanced over his shoulder. The metal dish lay on its side and, right behind it, the boy could see a gaping black hole in the floor.

The well was open.

Charlie listened. At first, the only thing he could hear was his own ragged breathing. Then he caught a noise, faint and far away. It sounded like drumming, but he knew now it was hoofbeats.

Mordred was coming.

The boy darted out of the vault and sped back through the tunnels. His arms and legs were pumping with all their might, but he concentrated on keeping his neck rigid, the beam of light steady and pointed down. If he stumbled and fell on the uneven floor, he would lose precious seconds, which might make the difference between life and death.

A blood-curdling roar echoed through the corridors behind him and, with a cry of fear, Charlie sprinted faster. Reaching the bottom of the steps, he scrabbled up, slipping on the wet stone, using his hands to propel himself forwards. But he was going too fast to judge distance properly. As he launched himself through the little hole at the top, his helmet cracked on the jagged brickwork and the light smashed, plunging him into utter blackness.

Charlie's bout of terrified swearing was drowned out by another monstrous bellow, much closer than the last. The boy scrambled to his feet and began stumbling along the corridor, one arm scraping along the wall, the other waving blindly in front. The best he could now manage was a hesitant shuffle. Mordred would catch him long before he reached the big top. He didn't even know how to get back now, for he couldn't see where the tunnels forked, never mind the chalked numbers telling him which passage to take.

He stopped, taking deep breaths, trying desperately to calm down. Wiping tears from his eyes, he peered into the blackness, in a vain attempt to see something, anything, that might give him a clue where the next turnoff lay.

And there it was. A glowing pinpoint of light punching a tiny hole in the darkness! Letting go of the wall, the boy staggered towards the glow, arms flailing in front of him, his stumbling run gathering momentum until it ended in a headlong dive. His lungs emptied with a painful whoosh as he landed heavily on the floor, outstretched fingers closing around a little sparkling object.

It was a juggling ball. Next to it was a handheld flashlight.

"Thank you, Lilly!" The boy switched on the torch. The beam lit up a numbered fork to his left. It was only two feet away.

There was another howl from Mordred, right behind Charlie. Then the boy was off again, racing up the passages, hurling himself around dark corners and crawling along the last narrow tunnel, like a jet-propelled mole. He burst into the maintenance vault, tearing the construction helmet from his head and flinging it across the room.

He could hear a horrific rending of stone, as something much larger and a thousand times stronger than he was, forced itself into the other end of the tunnel. Then Charlie was in the big top and racing for the exit, grasping Excalibur as he went past. The sword slid from the stone as easily as it had gone in and, seconds later, the boy was standing with his back to the theatre entrance, weapon held in front of his face.

The door that led to the workman's vault flew off its hinges with an explosion of shattered wood and Mordred stepped into the big top.

"Oh. My. God."

Charlie's face turned chalk white as he saw his opponent for the first time. Mordred was the height of a reasonably tall man, and there, any resemblance with humanity stopped. He had heavily muscled arms reaching almost to his knees and spade-like hands ended in a rash of vicious yellow talons. The creature's legs were short and thick and there were hooves where his feet should be. His body was maggot white, hairless and laced with thick blue veins.

But it was his face that shocked Charlie most. Mordred's angular head was bald and his jaw jutted forward like a mechanical scoop, lined with dozens of piranha-shaped teeth. His ears were disproportionately large, set flat against a smooth scalp, while the rest of his features were almost non-existent. The creature's nose was no more than a hole in the front of the face and his eyes had retreated far into his skull, two glowing points of hatred burning deep within waxy flesh.

Mordred took a few lurching steps towards the boy, raising his talons as he approached. Charlie lifted the sword over his head and pointed it towards the beast, like he had seen ninjas do in Kung Fu movies. He hoped it looked impressive.

"You're not getting past me. I don't care how big you are." He tried to sound bold and manly but the words came out as a series of trembling squeaks. "You never heard of David and Goliath?"

The monster halted. A strange gurgling sound rose from somewhere inside its chest and the jutting mouth split into a hideous upturned slash. Charlie realised, with growing horror, that the creature was laughing.

Then things got worse.

"Brave boy," the troll gurgled. "Even if you do hold the Great Sword."

Mordred's speech was thick and vibrant, buzzing like a swarm of feasting flies. Despite his terror, Charlie was surprised to notice the creature had a distinct Scottish accent.

He gripped the sword handle tighter and cleared his throat. It occurred to him that Mordred hadn't spoken to a human in two centuries and might be inclined to chat before tearing him limb from limb. Mordred looked around the big top with what Charlie presumed was a satisfied grin.

"You better go back where you came from before I chop you into bits," the boy croaked.

"Mordred cannot pass while you have the weapon, as you surely know," the creature hissed back. "But he does not need a door to escape. The poor walls of this dwelling are not like the thick stone of the prison where he suffered so long."

Mordred headed for the side of the big top, ignoring Charlie.

"He shall tear his way out with bare hands."

The boy kept quiet, Excalibur tight in his trembling fist. Mordred raised a taloned claw. Charlie held his breath.

The creature stopped, sniffing suspiciously at the air around the wall. He turned his white, mottled head and stared malevolently at his adversary. Hairs rose on the back of Charlie's neck.

"Clever. Soooo clever," the troll growled. "It is daylight outside, is it not? You have tried to fool Mordred, daring little fellow."

He cantered back over to the centre of the theatre, clicking sharp talons together, considering his situation.

"Smart little boy," he muttered. "But Mordred can wait for night to fall. After all, he has waited for fourteen centuries to be free. Can you imagine that?"

"Not really." Charlie shook his head.

"No. Mordred can hardly imagine it himself, nor does he want to." He hunkered down in the middle of the big top. "After such a time, he can pass a few more hours, heh?"

He laughed a bitter, gurgling laugh again.

"I'll fight you," Charlie said in a tiny voice. His legs were trembling so badly that he could hardly stand, and he felt sick and dizzy with fear. "Like you said, I have the sword."

"A Galhadrian is behind this," the creature whispered, tapping its head with a claw. "You would not dare do it on your own."

It clicked talons together again.

"Stalemate," it murmured. "Mordred fears Excalibur, that is true. Yet, you cannot catch him, for he is fast. He will wait."

"Hopefully, that will give you time to stop speaking about yourself in the third person." Charlie put on a false show of bravado. "It's really irritating."

The creature grinned, revealing three rows of teeth.

"At nightfall, Mordred shall simply slice his way through these puny walls to freedom." He began to plod towards the back of the theatre. "You cannot guard every inch."

"I don't intend to." Charlie looked up to make sure he was in the right position. Six feet above his head, the safety net for high wire acts stretched from one side of the big top to the other. He bent trembling knees, tensing the muscles in his body, then leapt into the air, slashing as high as the sword could reach.

Excalibur's blade swept through the steel ropes fastening the net to the wall as if they were thread. With a loud twang, one side of the mesh swept down, draping itself over Mordred.

Charlie charged forward with a yell, as the creature spun, snarling in anger. Though the safety net was made of wire and coated with toughened rubber, the creature's talons sliced through the mesh as easily as Excalibur had. Mordred's arm shot out and grasped one of the metal posts that roped off the performance area. He plucked it from the theatre floor as if it were a weed, the securing bolts popping out of the concrete like bullets.

He flung the spike at the boy.

Charlie dived as the post rocketed towards him, hunching his shoulders and tucking in his head, the way he had seen his parents do a hundred times. The metal bar whizzed past, inches over his hunched form and Charlie straightened out of the dive in time to see Mordred reaching for another post. With a grunt, he threw Excalibur straight at the creature.

Mordred roared in defiance and launched himself sideways, rolling as effectively as Charlie had done, though the movement tangled him even more in the safety net. Excalibur sliced harmlessly past and clattered to the back of the theatre.

Now the beast was between Charlie and his only weapon.

"The child has lost the Great Sword!" he cackled, slicing at the net again. "The child is lost too."

But, instead of turning back, Charlie headed straight for Mordred. The creature slashed wildly at the net, trying to free its arms properly and the jagged rows of teeth slavered as they bit down on the wire strands.

With every atom of his strength, Charlie leapt again, arms outstretched like a soaring bird, up over Mordred's head. The monster thrust one tangled arm skyward, claws glinting, but the boy tucked his head down again and flicked his legs up. With a grace and skill that would have delighted his parents, he twisted in the air. The boy arched over Mordred's outstretched arm, somersaulting perfectly and landing on his feet on the other side of the monster.

Momentum kept him going and he staggered to the back of the theatre, grabbed Excalibur from the floor, jumped and slashed again. The other side of the safety net pinged away from the wall and enveloped the creature once more. With a ferocious howl, Mordred tore into the new mesh folds with teeth and claws. They fell away like torn spider webs.

"Mordred will be free before you can reach him!" he crowed.

"I'm not coming near you." Charlie reached down to a prop table, half-hidden in the shadows, and picked up a small black box. He pointed it at the big top roof.

"Welcome to the 21st century," he said, the tremble gone from his voice.

He pressed a green button.

With an electronic whirr, the two halves of the theatre roof began to separate. Mordred's head shot up and he gave a wail as a line of sunlight appeared on the theatre floor. He struggled out of the net and lumbered towards the back of the theatre, but now Charlie and Excalibur stood between him and the only way back to the tunnels. Behind the creature, a widening band of light danced and sparkled on the chrome and plastic of the theatre fittings.

The monster looked at Charlie, clasping its clawed hands together, as if in prayer. Tiny eyes, filled now with sadness and fear, burned into the boy. Charlie felt a sharp pain in his chest.

For a fleeting second, he had seen something terribly human in that stare.

"Clever little fellow," Mordred whispered softly, as the sunlight reached him. "He is victorious."

Charlie's eyes widened. Watching the light hit Mordred was like witnessing some deformed snowman caught in an inferno. The troll dissolved in front of his eyes, gobbets of flesh sliding from its body, hissing and bubbling, the way fat melts in a pan. Turning his head upwards and stretching out his mighty arms, Mordred let out one last agonised roar.

"MORGANAAAAAAAAAAAAAAAAAAAAAAAA!"

The sound echoed round and round the big top, until the monster was gone, leaving nothing but a pool of rancid flesh on the floor.

Charlie dropped Excalibur, his chest heaving.

"Dad was right," he said morosely. "This trip has certainly brought me out of my shell."

Sinking to his knees, he began to cry.

The Thin Place

Charlie's palms hurt, though they had finally stopped bleeding. His tears had dried up too - and he sat quietly in the middle of the big top floor, looking like an exhausted clown. His face and hair were white from dust in the Underground City and the knees and elbows of his clothes were worn away by crawling through the tunnel. His dishevelled appearance fitted the surroundings perfectly. The door to the workmen's vault lay scattered in pieces across the floor, and so did bits of Mordred. There was a metal pole sticking out of one of the big top wall supports and the roof was gaping open to the sun.

The roof! Charlie leapt to his feet, pointed the remote control and clicked. With a grinding sound, the metal flanges, high above, closed again. Anyone outside would simply presume the mechanism was being tested. The boy looked at his watch and was surprised to see it was still only 6.30am. Good. Not many people would be about, especially in this quiet little street. Hopefully, Mordred's dying yell would be mistaken for the Geronimo-style roar of a practising acrobat.

The boy was so exhausted he could hardly think straight, but getting the hell out of this wrecked tent, undetected, certainly seemed a priority. He wondered where Lilly was.

He gave the control box for the big top roof a wipe with his T-shirt, in case the police were inclined to fingerprint it, prised Excalibur into the gap between the doorframe and the theatre door and sliced through the hasp of the lock. Now investigators might think the big top had been broken into and vandalised. Charlie wrapped the sword in the paint cloth and stuck his head nervously out of the door. Nobody was about. He hurried up the sunlit wynd and turned the corner onto the High Street without seeing another soul.

At this time in the morning, even the High Street was quiet and the few passers-by didn't pay much attention to Charlie's tousled hair and torn clothes. After all, the festival was filled with performers dressed in weird and wonderful costumes to promote their shows. Right now there was a lone figure dressed as a penguin plodding down the other side of the road.

He had to figure out what to do with Excalibur. The sword was worth a fortune, he had no doubt, but what use was that to him? If he tried to sell it, there would be all sorts of very awkward questions, like what was a young boy doing with a two-thousand-year-old sword made of a metal science couldn't explain? If Lilly was right, a magic blade wasn't meant for human eyes any more than Mordred had been.

The fairest thing the boy could think of was to put Excalibur back where he found it. The graveyard was bound to be empty at this time of day. He could go straight there, replace the sword and be back in bed before his parents woke up. Tucking Excalibur under his arm, he headed for Greyfriars.

When he arrived, there was a small figure standing outside the wrought-iron gates, pressed against the wall as if trying to stay hidden from anyone in the cemetery.

"Lilly?"

"Get over here." Lilly motioned nervously to him. When he got close enough, she reached out and pulled him away from the gates. "Are you OK?"

"Mordred's dead." Charlie tapped his hand on the paint cloth, sharing credit with the hidden weapon.

"I guessed that, otherwise you wouldn't be standing here." She clasped the boy's arm and hugged him triumphantly. "You are something else, know that?"

"Thank you," Charlie blushed. There was so much white dust caked on his face that Lilly didn't notice.

"Where are you going now?" she whispered. "Are you going to put Excalibur back?"

"I am," the boy said miserably. "There goes my yacht."

"Not so loud!" Lilly hissed. "Listen. It's all very noble, what you're doing, but it's not a great idea for you to go in there."

"Why not? I've been before."

"Exactly!" Lilly glanced around nervously. "You saw a white hawk with black-tipped wings and there's no doubt it saw you."

"So?" Charlie screwed up his face. "I'm not a dormouse."

"The hawk is a lookout." Lilly scanned the clear blue sky. "For us. For the Little People! Greyfriars is a Thin Place, Charlie. You know what that is?"

"I remember from Peazle's diary." The boy thought for a second. "It's a place where the line between this world and Galhadria is almost non-existent."

"I presume my people let the sword lie hidden in Greyfriars in the hope someone would, someday, use it to defeat Mordred. Yet they are determined to remain a secret to humans."

Lilly tugged at the paint cloth.

"What do you think will happen if you go waltzing back in there now? They'll know you've killed him."

"So soon?"

"You're still alive, aren't you? Plus, you've got bits of troll stuck to your boots."

"Oh, yeah." Charlie looked down. "Think that'll come off?"

"Even worse, you worked out who I am." The girl looked at him imploringly. "You go in there and you'll never come out again."

Charlie scowled.

"You Galhadrians aren't exactly big on gratitude, are you?"

"No, we're not." It was Lilly's turn to go red. "As you so perceptively put it, we aren't big on anything except dancing, singing and enjoying ourselves. Helping others isn't high on our agenda."

"Why don't you take the sword in for me, then?" The boy held out the weapon.

"I can't!" Lilly stepped back. "My people don't approve of me hanging around on earth. If I set foot in a Thin Place, they might force me back to Galhadria with them."

"What's wrong with that?" The boy pushed the sword towards her again. "You've put right what your father did wrong. Well, you used me to put it right."

"I had to Charlie!"

"I understand." He patted her arm. "But while I'm being blunt...." He looked apologetic. "I don't think your father is ever coming back."

"Neither do I," Lilly replied sadly. "I hoped someday he might return to rescue his followers." A sudden cold wind rustled through the gate. "But I've gotten to quite like it here and, as you reminded me, we Galhadrians aren't big on gratitude."

"Well, I am." Charlie tucked the weapon back under his arm. "And I'm putting Excalibur back where it belongs."

He pushed at the gate and the iron lattice swung open with a creak.

Lilly hesitated, then stepped away from the wall. She fished in her pocket, brought out a small silver whistle and handed it to him.

"If you're ever in trouble. I mean real trouble, just blow. I'll be there for you, I promise."

"What about your no interfering with people rule?"

"I'd say it was a bit late for that. Besides, I owe you."

"I think I know why you want to stay on earth." The boy grinned and gave her a knowing wink. "After all this time, you're more human than Galhadrian."

"And you're more magical than any person I ever met. In all sorts of ways."

She threw her arms around the boy. He held her awkwardly with one arm, the other still clutching the paint cloth.

"Goodbye Charlie." She kissed his cheek. "I hope we'll meet again."

Lilly turned and ran. Halfway down the street, she gave a small skip.

Charlie watched her, heading further and further into the distance, until she looked just like any other girl in the world.

The shovel was where Charlie had left it, lying next to James Hogg's grave. The boy unwrapped Excalibur and stood over the denuded area where, the day before, he had scraped away the soil. There was a large flat rock, half-hidden under dirt, probably a remnant of some headstone that had fallen over and been covered. But the boy knew Excalibur's power and plunged the sword down anyway. It sank easily into the stone and the packed earth below, up to its hilt. Charlie hoped it hadn't gone through the remains of poor old James Hogg as well. He bent over to pick up the shovel. Once he had covered the handle, Excalibur would remain hidden for many years. Perhaps centuries.

"My goodness, there's an old friend," a voice said at his ear.

Charlie almost fell over. Two boys were standing behind him. One was short and thin, the other tall and muscular with long black hair. But it was their clothes that gave Charlie the biggest start. The short boy was wearing a bright yellow waistcoat, plus fours and a bowler hat and the taller one was resplendent in full highland regalia.

"We wanted to give you a proper welcome," said the bowler hat. "So we dressed up in our finest togs."

"Aye, we didnae want tae scare you," added the one in the kilt.

Having just won hand-to-hand combat with a vicious monster, Charlie was more astonished than alarmed. He simply stared, his mouth hanging open.

The shorter boy stepped forward.

"The name's Peazle," he said, "And this is my friend Duncan." He shook Charlie's unresisting hand. "Pleased to make your acquaintance."

"I know who you are." Charlie's face twisted into an incredulous smile. "I recognise you."

He let go of Peazle's hand.

"I can't believe this. Are you ghosts? You feel solid enough."

"Oh, we're real," Duncan laughed and Peazle giggled as well.

"How can that be?" The boy was as delighted as he was mystified.

"It's quite a… eh… strange explanation," Peazle said. "I take it you read the diary?"

Charlie nodded.

"What did you think of the writing style? You can be honest."

"Peazle!" The highlander glowered at his friend. "Just tell the story."

"Yes. Sorry. Well, when we beat the Gorrodin-Rath…" Peazle hooked both thumbs into the waistcoat in preparation for his tale.

"Most of the Gorrodin-Rath," Duncan broke in, nodding graciously at Charlie. The boy beamed with pride.

"Most of the Gorrodin-Rath," Peazle continued. "Anyway, we came here afterwards to bury the sword."

"Even Shadowjack?"

"Aye, he tagged along too." The boys from the past looked at each other knowingly.

"Peazle was dying of the ague," Duncan said solemnly. "And the wound I received from the falling rock was more serious than it first appeared. I think Shadowjack intended to wait until we were not fit tae resist, then dig the sword up again. I admit I was for selling it myself and buying my friend here some precious time. Yet Peazle wouldnae hear of it."

"What happened?" Charlie sat down on a headstone, enthralled. He was going to hear the end of Peazle's and Duncan's story at last.

"We buried the sword and were about tae go," Duncan began. "When we were surrounded by a group of Little People."

"And they're not so little," Peazle broke in. "Let me tell you that, for nothing."

"With Excalibur under the earth, we had no way tae defend ourselves," Duncan continued. "They took us back to Galhadria, Shadowjack as well - though he wasnae best pleased about it. We've been there ever since."

"But you're still young."

"That's the great thing about living in an enchanted realm," Peazle smiled. "Long life and good health. I've had two hundred years to study, more than anyone on earth. I always wanted to be a man of learning."

The pickpocket sat on the tomb next to Charlie and put his arm around the boy's shoulder.

"There's so much I want to discuss with you. I'm particularly interested in mapping genomes and DNA splicing." Peazle's eyes were bright with excitement. "How broad is your knowledge of genetic engineering?

You must have seen programmes about it on your marvellous invention, the television?"

"Not unless they made it into a cartoon."

Peazle grunted. Charlie turned to Duncan.

"What have *you* been up to for two hundred years?"

"Looking for my brother."

There was a long, uncomfortable silence.

"The Galhadrians claim to have nae knowledge of him." The highlander said coldly. "I search their land anyway."

Charlie removed Peazle's arm from his shoulder and stood up.

"What are you both doing here?" he asked warily.

"Like us, you know too much about the existence of the Little People for them to allow you to roam free on earth." Duncan's expression was impossible to read. "We've been sent to bring you back with us to Galhadria."

"I'd rather not, actually." The boy backed away.

"They thought we would be the best ones to fetch you," Peazle said sheepishly. "It's not so bad there, really. Galhadria is beautiful and I owe the Little People my life. They're courteous enough to us and don't interfere in our lives."

The boy was talking rapidly, trying to convince himself as much as Charlie.

"There are rivers and mountains for Duncan and books for me to read, and we can look after you."

"Not a chance." The boy shook his head vehemently. "I don't want to sound mean, but you were both orphans living in poverty. I actually have a life."

"Charlie, if you don't come with us, they'll take you themselves."

"Then they'll have a fight on their hands." Charlie spat. "I'm out of here."

"ENOUGH!"

The voice was low and clear and seemed to come from thin air. There was a bright shimmer around Hogg's grave, like a heat haze, and then the area behind the tomb seemed to rupture. A narrow shaft of blue light split the fabric of the air and a stranger stepped through it and into the graveyard.

He was tall and slender, with red hair cascading around an angular face. Piercing green eyes matched his emerald tunic and he wore a green kilt with a short sword fastened to his thick leather belt.

"That's Jack Thane," Peazle whispered. "One of Galhadrians greatest Sorcerers."

"The hour grows late," Thane said, bowing politely to Charlie. "Soon, humans will begin to enter this place."

His hand whipped out at lightning speed and grabbed the boy's arm. The fingers gripped like iron and a bone-deep numbness spread from Charlie's elbow to wrist.

"You have done us a great service and will be treated well, yet your fate cannot be altered. You must come with me."

Duncan and Peazle looked at each other and hung their heads.

"Take the sword back to Galhadria, highlander," the stranger instructed Duncan. "That is where we all belong now."

With a glowering look at the Galhadrian, Duncan bent over, grabbed Excalibur's hilt and pulled. The sword didn't budge. The highlander planted his feet firmly on the ground, put both hands around the handle and pulled until he was red in the face. He gave up and stepped back, dumbfounded.

"It winnae move," he said.

"What?" The Galhadrian let go of Charlie. "Stay there."

He walked around the flat tombstone to where the sword handle protruded from the soil. Charlie looked at the graveyard gate. It was a hundred yards away, half-hidden by the church and he had no doubt Thane could catch him long before he got there.

The wizard stood over Hogg's grave, clutching the sword. Charlie shuffled a few steps towards the flat tombstone and, as he did so, caught Peazle's eye. The pickpocket shook his head slowly, warning the boy not to try anything. Charlie held his gaze. Peazle shook his head again. Charlie shaped his mouth into one unspoken word.

Please.

Peazle bit his lip, then nodded. Duncan caught the silent exchange and, without a change of expression, edged closer to his friend.

The Galhadrian was pulling with all his might on the handle of Excalibur, but the sword had not moved an inch. He stood up, the exertion on his face changing to incredulity.

"How did you achieve this?" He stepped onto the flat tomb and towered over the boy. "What have you done?"

"Now!" Peazle shouted - and he and Duncan leapt. The boys hit Thane with a flying tackle and all three tumbled off the tombstone in a tangle of arms and legs. Charlie launched himself forward, cartwheeling over the gravestone, landing in a crouch on the other side. He grabbed the sword handle and pulled Excalibur out of the ground with one fluid motion. The Galhadrian swept Duncan and Peazle away as if they were toys. He was on his feet in an instant, face contorted with rage.

Charlie pointed the sword at his chest.

"I've already killed one magical creature today," he snarled. "Do you want to be the second?"

Thane was barely listening. He stood transfixed, staring at the sword in the boy's hand. Duncan and Peazle struggled to their feet, equally astounded. They had expected Charlie to run for the exit.

"You took the sword from the stone," the Galhadrian said, awe in his voice. "When I could not."

"So what?" Excalibur did not waver in the boy's hand. "Is this a trick?"

"Excalibur has a power of its own," Thane said. "It will not let me wield it… and yet you can. I do not understand."

He held up his hand in a gesture of truce.

"Perhaps some of the Gorrodin-Rath still live. Or you have formed a bond with the weapon, for reasons I do not yet comprehend. Whatever the cause, Excalibur's work is not done here and, therefore, neither is yours."

"Really?" Charlie snorted. "I think I've done all the work I'm going to do for you."

"That is your choice." The wizard bowed low. "But the sword will remain here, in case you need it someday. You may bury it and return to your world. I will not interfere."

Charlie looked at Peazle and Duncan.

"His word is good," said Duncan. "I'll vouch for that, at least."

"I trust you will not speak of this," Thane glowered at the boy. "Or I shall return and your punishment will be great."

"My lips are sealed." The boy lowered Excalibur. The air around the grave had begun to shimmer again.

"Then, farewell Master Wilson." The wizard motioned curtly to Peazle and Duncan.

"Come," he said brusquely, stepping into the light without a backwards glance.

Duncan smiled at the boy.

"Good luck Charlie." He hesitated, then followed the wizard through the gateway to Galhadria. Peazle stopped at the entrance to the light.

"Until we meet again, my friend." He doffed his hat and vanished into Galhadria.

Charlie saluted him with his sword until the shimmer in the air faded away.

Charlie's mother and father were sitting on a couch eating breakfast, when their son walked into the guestroom. The boy's hair was matted with dust and grime, his mud-spattered clothes were ripped and dirty and there was a large bloodstain down one side of his shirt.

"What on earth happened to you?" his mother said, dropping her spoon. "Are you all right?"

"I've been practising." The boy plonked himself on a chair between his parents and put an arm around each of them. "I want you to teach me to be an acrobat."

His parents stared at him, then at each other.

"Well, that's great, Charlie," his father said, unable to keep the pride out of his voice. He patted his son tentatively on the back. "In fact, it's fantastic!"

"We'd be delighted, Charlie." His mother smiled at him warmly. "There's plenty of stuff to learn, but we'll start whenever you like."

"I've had a hard day." The boy let go of his parents, sank back wearily and closed his eyes. A slow smile spread across his face.

"But tomorrow? I think I'll start with a bit of juggl-ing."

Epilogue

187

Deep in a cavern, far to the north, a creature stirred, misshapen ears pricking up on its hairless head. From far away, the cry of her dying kin, born on wind and wave, wafted down to wreck her centuries-long slumber.

One tiny eye opened in a mass of white flesh.

Morgana was awake.

END

Book One of the Galhadrian Trilogy

ABOUT THE AUTHOR

Jan-Andrew Henderson (J.A. Henderson) is the author of 40 children's, teen, YA, adult and non-fiction books. Published in the UK, USA, Australia, Canada and Europe, he has been shortlisted for fifteen literary awards and won the Doncaster Book Prize, the Aurealis Award and the Royal Mail Award.

www.janandrewhenderson.com

www.ingramcontent.com/pod-product-compliance
Lightning Source LLC
Chambersburg PA
CBHW020330110726
47898CB00003B/823